HALLOWEEN
SEASON

Published by Raw Dog Screaming Press
Bowie, MD
All rights reserved.
First Edition

Book design: Jennifer Barnes
Cover art copyright 2020 by Lynne Hansen
LynneHansenArt.com

Printed in the United States of America
ISBN: 9781947879218

Library of Congress Control Number: 2020941836

www.RawDogScreaming.com

HALLOWEEN
SEASON

Lucy A. Snyder

RAW DOG
SCREAMING
PRESS

Acknowlededgments

I'd like to thank Jennifer Barnes and the staff at Raw Dog Screaming Press for all their hard work on this book. I'd also like to thank the editors who first purchased or commissioned the stories collected here: Jennifer Brozek, Alex Shvartsman, Doug Murano, Douglas Draa, Kerrie L. Hughes, Christopher M. Jones, Kenneth W. Cain, Robert S. Wilson, Gavin Grant, and Kelly Swails. I'd also like to thank my beta readers for their keen eyes, valuable insights, and unflagging support: Gary A. Braunbeck, Mark Freeman, Michael Lucas, and Scott Slemmons.

And finally, I'd like to thank my Patreon supporters for helping to make this book a reality: *Abyss & Apex Magazine*, Alex Harford, Amanda Hoffelt-Ryan, Anita Siraki, Anne Marie Lutz, Anthony R. Cardno, Anthony Klancar, Arasibo Campeche, Benjamin Holesapple, Brittany Marschalk, Carie Martin, Carol Baker, Christine Lucas, Cristina D. Ramirez, Deanne Fountaine, Donna Munro, Dora Knez, Elizabeth Bennefeld, Elizabeth Donald, Emma Munro, Eric Grizzle, Eric Sprague, Evan Dicken, Ferrett Steinmetz, Hanna Brady, Heather Munn, Holly Zaldivar, Human People, Ingrid de Beus, J. Thorne, Jennifer Covel, Jim Leach, Joanna Weston, Jodi Davis, Joe Haldeman and Gay Haldeman, Joel Kramer, Juliana McCorison, Julie Megchelsen, Kerry Adrienne, Kira Barnes, Kyndall Elliott, Laurent Castellucci, librarista, Linda Addison, Lisa Morton, Lorena Haldeman, Margaret Steurer, Martha Wells, Michael Cieslak, Molly DePriest, Neil Flinchbaugh, Querus Abuttu, Rebecca Allred, Roberta Slocumb, Sarah Hans, Scott A. Johnson, Shannon Eichorn, S.L. Ember, Stephanie Heminger, Tanith Korravai, Tom Smith, Victoria Fredrick, and Weston Kincade.

Contents

Beggars' Night 9

Hazelnuts and Yummy Mummies................................. 11

Cosmic Cola.. 23

Visions of the Dream Witch... 47

What Dwells Within 61

The Porcupine Boy.. 83

In the Family 99

The Kind Detective 106

A Preference For Silence 115

Wake Up Naked Monkey You're Going to Die............ 118

The Great VüDü Teen Linux Zombie Massacree........... 122

The House That Couldn't Clean Itself......................... 131

After Hours 142

The Toymaker's Joy.. 143

The Tingling Madness 152

Beggars' Night

Stinky kid sneakers peek beneath
ghostly sheets and shredded zombie jeans.
Chatty moms herd sugarbuzzed superheroes
and tween princesses off strangers' lawns
onto frosty concrete to await safe treats.

But half past nine, flashlight batteries die,
buzzing streetlamps flicker to silent black
as scudding clouds blot the gibbous moon;
manly hearts jump as small sweaty fingers
impatiently twist free from daddies' hands.

And in the sudden dark, for just a moment,
cheap cotton gauze spins to Egyptian linen,
latex and greasepaint become twitching scars,
hairy feral muscle splits wispy nylon rags,
and every smile stinks of clotted blood.

But in a heartbeat, the dire clouds retreat,
the moon shines brave and the lamps relight.
Trembling parents retrieve little tricksters,
ruffle hair, press hands to narrow chests,
unable to feel the monsters burning inside.

Hazelnuts and Yummy Mummies

I was at the edge of the SowenCon Author Alley in the main vendor hall when the drugs began to take hold. A guy in a black Batman tee shirt was frowning down at my books, clearly not liking what he saw. I'd nailed a smile to my face as I chatted about the plot of my first novel, but I knew I wasn't connecting because his scowl deepened and deepened but he wasn't walking away so I started babbling about the plot of the rest of the series while thinking, *Oh god, why did I agree to do this?*

You agreed to this because they offered you a free hotel room and you have to stay busy this weekend, my Inner Responsible Adult replied. *On Halloween, you have to stay busy. You* have *to, or you will think too many thoughts and end up in the bin again.*

Keeping busy was good. But I wasn't any kind of plausible saleswoman. Nobody was going to hire me to pitch jewelry or juicers. I became a writer in the first pea-picking place because I could only seem to gather my thoughts on paper; I constantly found myself tongue-tied whenever I had to meet new people. So why in the name of sweet candy corn was I working a table trying to talk up books I'd written precisely because I could never reliably form complete sentences except with a keyboard? Couldn't I have chosen to stay busy doing something less painful, like competing in ghost pepper eating contests? Nude sandpaper surfing? Milking angry sharks?

In my mind, I heard my dead mother's voice: "Life is a grand comedy, dear; just do your best."

I suddenly felt too hot despite the chilly diesel-stinky October draft from the loading dock in back and my head felt floaty and puffy like a party balloon. And I wasn't even sure what words were coming out of my mouth. *Something something* action *something* adventure *something* award-winning *something.* Batfan's face scrunched up more and more, getting impossibly wrinkled, and his nose squinched and flattened and inverted, his eyes shrunk tiny, black and beady and suddenly I was looking up at the head of an actual bat. A brown bat like the ones that roosted under the overpass near my mom's house back in Missouri. Except fifty times as huge, because brown bats are itty-bitty and the Batfan had a noggin the size of a cantaloupe.

I trailed off, gaping at him. *What. The. Actual. Fuck.*

And then wondered: *Did I say that out loud?*

The bat gave me a weird, suspicious look and walked away without a screech.

Elaine, the SowenCon author liaison, came hurrying up, her tall pointy witch hat askew, her glittery blue satin dress swirling and glowing like galaxies. Her whole outfit seemed to have turned into a portal to another dimension. I felt as though I might fall right into it.

"Miss Bowen?" she said. By her expression, it wasn't the first time she'd tried to get my attention. A halo of stardust seemed to float around her face.

"Yes?" I replied. My tongue felt too big in my mouth. It seemed huge as a tuna, and it might wriggle free and go swimming across the sea-green carpet. I'd have to chase it down in the gaming room, tackle it near the Munchkin tournament. The idea of that made me laugh out loud.

"Did you eat one of the black raspberry cookies?" Elaine was frowning, looking worried. Her face was getting wrinkled up. I wondered if she was going to turn into a bat, too.

She'd been by a half-hour before with a big basket of homemade Halloween cookies for all the guest authors and artists. A whole spread of tiny frosted tombstones, snickerdoodle ghosts, gingerbread cats. And black cookies, each decorated with a single blue candy eye. I have blue eyes, and after three hours of sitting at my table, the thought of devouring my own flesh had started to appeal to me. So I took two, and gave one to my friend Heather, who'd come with me to the convention to help schlep books and maintain my sanity.

"Did you eat one of the black cookies?" Elaine repeated.

I nodded slowly. "It was tasty. But the frosting was a little bitter."

"Oh no." She leaned in over by books. "Listen. I meant to give you a treat, but you got a trick by mistake. You've just consumed a fairly large dose of a hallucinogen. Those black cookies were for our ritual tonight, but our initiate got the batches mixed up."

Elaine's eyes were swirling, glittering, dark as a black pearl ring my mom used to own. It was always her favorite. She lost it in the ocean the same day she got her first diagnosis.

"My mom died five years ago today," I blurted out. "She had two kinds of cancer and ehrlichiosis and cryptosporidium and it all killed her. It was like watching Boromir get shot with those black arrows. She never did *anything* halfway, not even dying."

"I'm…I'm really sorry to hear that. But the hallucinogen—"

"On Halloween we're supposed to remember the dead," I said. "But how can I not remember my mom dying? How could I ever *not* think about that? So she could have died any other day and I'd still remember. Dying on Halloween was just…overkill. But hey, that's Mom! Never do things halfway."

"I'm truly sorry about your mother, but *listen!*" Elaine was speaking very slowly and clearly, as if she were addressing a learning-disabled child. "The hallucinogen is going to give you visions. It might last five or six hours."

I had a moment of rational clarity: "I take antidepressants. There's a bunch of stuff I'm not supposed to take with them. Is the cookie going to make me sick?"

"I don't think so." She sounded profoundly uncertain, and her voice echoed as if she were in a large cavern. "Many of us in the coven are also on antidepressants and nobody's had a problem. But you do need to drink a lot of water. I'm going to call someone to take you back to your hotel room and keep an eye on you. I'll get someone else to watch your table for the rest of the day. Everything will be fine."

"I have a panel on zombie poetry in an hour," I said, watching tiny stardust pixies dance around her hat.

"Don't worry about the panel—"

"But I have to warn them." I gazed up at her, suddenly realizing it was not merely another convention panel but a very important personal mission. "I have to warn them all that when you write poetry, you are letting the brain eaters into your mind. You are letting them into your mind!"

"Listen, don't worry about the brain eaters. Just come around the table take my hand and we'll get you back to your room and get you some blankets and water, and—"

"VICTORIAAAA!"

Heather was zooming down the carpeted aisle full-speed on her electric, candy apple red mobility scooter. Startled con-goers were dodging right and left to get out of her way. She'd had surgery on both feet four weeks earlier and while she'd been okayed to walk short distances, the vastness of the convention center was just too much.

Her eyes were hugely dilated, and she had a sweaty look of determination I seldom saw outside end game rounds of Iron Dragon. In her free arm, she clutched a brand-new skateboard decorated with the colorful unicorn logo of one of the role-playing game companies that was sponsoring the convention. As far as I knew, she didn't skateboard and certainly wasn't in any condition to do it now. Had she bought it? Won it? *Stolen* it? Was this Grand Theft Skateboard?

She plunked it down on the floor beside my table as though she were throwing a gauntlet. "Victoria! The Ghost of Trick-or-Treat needs us!"

"It does?"

"Yes! Come with me if you want to save The Great Pumpkin!" Her words rang with irresistible authority. I was needed. Summoned. *Destined.*

Nervous purple fairies orbited Elaine's head. "I don't think—"

"OK!" I jumped up and stared down at the skateboard, which was undulating slightly, like a cat that was about to hork up a hairball. "What now?"

"Get upon this flatfish steed and grab the back of my Harley!"

I was sure that the skateboard might vomit all over my shoes, but a good soldier in the Halloween army honors the call of duty. I stepped on the wobbly board and grasped the back of the scooter's seat. The black vinyl bubbled up between my fingers and hissed at me, but I held fast.

"Oh, Miss Bowen, no—"

"To infinity!" Heather punched the scooter into high gear.

We zoomed past the laughing liquid racks of vendors' books and games, faster and faster, the colors streaking and boiling with sparks as we approached light speed. And then with a blast of outer space cold, we were in the Haunter's Hall where cartoon ghosts whooshed above the bloated foam animatronic zombies and shrieking funhouse mansion-fronts. Heather's speeding wheels kicked up a storm of autumn leaves that made me sneeze from the smell of wood smoke and pumpkin spice. The leaves swirled up around us in a rattling vortex of reds and oranges and browns, their brittle serrated edges lashing my face and arms, and I let go of the scooter to shield my eyes—

—the skateboard squirted out from beneath my feet and my arms windmilled as I fell forward through empty darkness—

—and I face-planted onto someone's frosty lawn, the air whoofing out of my lungs.

"Clumsy," a man above me said. "A princess shouldn't be clumsy."

I pushed myself up onto my knees. My arms were tiny, and I was wearing a pink princess outfit made from cheap satin and stiff crinoline with stars made from glue and silver and pink glitter. The dress was loose. I'd outgrown this costume when I was five or six, and my mom gave it to Goodwill.

I looked up at the man, whose face was obscured by mist. The only thing I could see clearly was the Budweiser longneck in a blue koozie in his right hand.

"Papa?" I asked uncertainly. Mom had burned all his photos after he left us when I was five, and all I could really remember about him was the beer he always seemed to have. But before he decided fatherhood and marriage weren't for him, he had taken me trick-or-treating when Mom was attending night classes after her waitressing shifts to become a computer operator. It was possibly the least he could do. But he did it.

"Well, get up, Whoopsy-Daisy, and let's get you some candy." My father held out his free hand, helped me to my feet, and picked dead leaves off my dress.

Decades later, during an online search, I learned that he died in a drunk driving accident in Mexico about two years after he left us. If Mom knew about that, she never let on. She'd been so furious and hurt that not only did she destroy all evidence of his existence in the house, she changed both our last names back to her maiden name. Alex Ronson had given me nothing that lasted except some DNA and a couple of hazy memories.

If he'd sobered up, he might have called or written me. He might have come back and tried to be a father. A lot of things could have happened, but of course they didn't. The brief article I'd found just listed his expiration date and the cause; it didn't say if he'd died instantly in his smashed fast car or if he'd lingered in pain in the hospital as my mother had.

"Did it hurt?" I asked him.

"Did what hurt?" he grunted as he led me up the sidewalk of our old neighborhood toward Mrs. Robinson's house. She always had the best candies for trick-or-treaters: full-sized Kit-Kats and peanut butter cups and Almond Joys.

"When you died," I said. "Did it hurt?"

"No, it didn't hurt at all."

His voice had changed. I looked up, and saw the man was now my mom's boyfriend Joe Moreno. He looked the same as he had when he was thirty or so: angular face softened by his gentle brown eyes, his thick black hair parted down the middle and feathered back like it was still 1988. He worked as an ER nurse. He met my mom when I was seven, and they stayed together until he suffered a massive heart attack in the hospital parking lot and died.

He took a long drag from his Lucky Strike and puffed smoke rings into the chilly autumn air. "Well, that's a little lie. It was the worst crushing cramp in my chest you can imagine, but my knees buckled and I fell and cracked my head on a concrete parking block. Knocked me clean out, and I didn't feel anything after that. They found me quick and brought me back into the ER; it took me maybe a half hour to die while they were working hard on me. They busted nearly every rib and I didn't feel it. As deaths go, mine was totally ironic, but I got off easy pain-wise."

"I'm sorry," I said, gripping his warm hand more tightly. "You were only forty-five, and it wasn't fair."

"Don't be sorry. I got to help a lot of people at the hospital. Save little kids. I got to be *worthy*. And I had a good life with Donna, and after a while I thought of you as my own daughter. Even if I always told you to call me Joe. I did my best to be a good dad, but I never figured I had the right to claim to be your father unless Donna and me got married, and we didn't."

I blinked, surprised at the regret in his voice. "I thought you never wanted to?"

Another, longer drag, and more smoke rings. The smell of his tobacco in the air made my heart ache at how much I'd missed his calm, steady strength in my life the past thirteen years. He was the perfect balance to my mom's passionate volatility and he'd mediated plenty of arguments between her and me. Without him around, not much could stop Hurricane Donna. I loved my mom and I knew she loved me, but when I had the chance to move across the country for a job, I took it. And, later, I lay awake at night wondering if my absence meant she hadn't gone to the doctor when she needed to.

"I thought about marriage plenty," Joe said, "but things were good the way they were, you know? Marriage changes things; it's like a mutation. Sometimes your relationship gets superpowers, but sometimes it goes malignant. I didn't want to risk the good thing we had. And neither did your mom, not after the ways your dad changed."

If Joe had lived, he might have spotted signs of Mom's cancer earlier when it was still treatable. He would have been able to go with her to appointments and advocate for better care.

If he'd lived, maybe they'd both still be alive.

"You were always good to us," I told him. "I'll never forget that."

Joe smiled around his cigarette. "That's the best thing an old ghost like me can hope for."

I felt myself grow bigger as he led me to Mrs. Robinson's house. By the time we reached the front door, I was adult-sized again and my princess dress was gone, replaced by my usual outfit of jeans and a black tee shirt. Joe pulled open the screen door so I could knock.

After two raps, the door swung inward, but it wasn't Mrs. Robinson's living room. It was the cluttered den in my mom's sister Catherine's split-level in Maine. The smells of warm apple cider and popcorn wafted from the kitchen. My aunt's six-year-old twins Noah and Natalie had dressed up as pirates and were shrieking with glee and chasing each other around the room with foam cutlasses.

I hadn't seen Catherine since my mom's funeral; the twins were still in diapers, and she'd left them at home with her husband. She only stayed for the funeral and reception. Seven hours at the most, and then she was back in the air. I'd only seen her kids in photos and videos on Facebook, but they looked like a real handful for a couple of fortysomethings. Somewhere I read that older mother's kids inherited weakened mitochondria, but Noah and Natalie seemed to have enough energy to power an entire city.

"I'm not taking you trick-or-treating if you don't calm down and put on your coats!" Catherine yelled.

I tried to take a step forward into the house, but found myself blocked by an invisible wall.

"Just as well," I muttered. "They don't know me anyhow."

"They *could* know you," Joe said. "You could be there right now."

I shook my head. "She didn't have much time for me before Mom died, and later…well, she acted all weird after I tried to kill myself. Acted like…like the crazy would rub off on her or something. Facebook's as close as she wants me, I guess."

"She did say to visit any time."

"Yeah, but…come on, she didn't mean that. She was just trying to be polite."

"She can't know that you even want to visit if you don't try. And your cousins won't remember you if they never get to see you."

"It's too hard." I stared down at my black Chuck Taylors, still dusted with purple and silver glitter from the princess dress. "I can't put myself out there and have her reject me again. I just can't."

The light dimmed. I looked up, and realized that Joe and I were standing in a cramped efficiency apartment between a drab brown couch and a flatscreen TV tuned to a cheesy 50s horror movie. The room stank of spilled beer, garbage, and unwashed laundry. A sallow-eyed woman in a blue bathrobe was sitting on the couch, blankly staring past us at the screen; she didn't seem to know we were there. Her face was bloated, and so it took me a second to realize that the woman was *me*. A broken-down me 15 or 20 years in the future, fifty pounds heavier with an alcoholic's reddened skin. This was surely what giving up looked like.

"Well, shit," I whispered.

The coffee table in front of her was cluttered with empty bottles of Budweiser and cheap whiskey along with crumpled Taco Bell and Halloween candy wrappers. She pushed through the mess until she found a mostly-full bottle of Wild Turkey and a bottle of Tylenol. The sad woman started tossing back the painkillers by the handful, washing them down with the whiskey.

"Fuck, no, stop!" I stepped toward her, but the invisible wall blocked me again.

"She'll be dead in days," Joe said. "I saw my share of people who decided to commit suicide like this. It's effective, cheap, and an awful way to die. The alcohol and acetaminophen turns your liver to dog food. There's no help for it except an emergency transplant, and almost nobody can get that. Not without money, and…well. Doesn't look like there's much of that around here."

I pressed the heels of my hands against my eyes. "Shit."

When I dropped my hands, Joe and I were standing in a darkened hospital corridor. It seemed familiar, but I couldn't quite place it. Hospitals all look pretty much the same. The walls were decorated with cardboard Halloween witches, pumpkins, and black cats. Most of the rooms were dark and their doors closed, but the light was on in one open room toward the end of the hall.

"I'm sorry you didn't get any trick-or-treat goodies." Joe reached into the pocket of his windbreaker and pulled out a colorful package of candy. "Here you go."

I took the proffered pack. The cartoon ancient Egyptian on the wrapper gripped a blue Tropical Fruit Punch mummy that looked more like a board he was going to use to surf some dunes. "Yummy Mummies? Really?"

Joe shrugged and grinned. "Hey, I'm stuck in 1988, what did you expect?"

His grin faded and he nodded toward the lighted room. "You should go see her now."

My stomach churned. "Is…is Mom in there?"

"She is."

"I…I can't." I shook my head. I couldn't go back to that night. It was my worst failure. I *couldn't.*

"Vicky, I can't make you. But you know what happens if you don't try. The guilt will keep eating you from the inside out."

"Okay." I took a deep breath. "Okay."

I tucked the pack of Yummy Mummies into my back pocket and slowly walked down the hall to my mom's room. My dread increased with every step. I'd had nightmares about this nearly every week for the past five years, and now I had to face her.

She lay mute and too sick to move in the bed, just as I remembered her. And the smell—the hospital antiseptic overlaying the stink of diarrhea and vomit made me want to gag. The veins in her arms had collapsed and she'd gone into kidney failure, so they had stuck a quiver of painful-looking needles into the pulsing vessels in her neck to hook her up to various IV tubes. One was for saline, another for an antiparasitic drug, and the rest for dialysis. The surgical tape over the needles hadn't held properly and blood had slowly seeped out in a sticky, uncomfortable-looking pool spreading across the hollows of her collarbones and down her cleavage. Futile silver bags hung on the IV tree above her.

And I—the five-years-younger version of me—sat in the chair beside her. Staring at her with a dazed expression. Just staring and watching her die.

"C'mon," I begged myself. "Get up and call a nurse to come sponge her off. *Get up.*"

But I couldn't hear myself and just kept sitting and staring. I know what I was thinking. The nurses during the day had buzzed around my mother with impatient efficiency and I'd just tried to stay out of their way. At night, I hadn't been able to shift to realizing that now nobody else was checking on her and I needed to do something. But I felt like a bystander, an observer. I felt helpless in the face of all those needles and tubes and malignant cells I couldn't stop. It never occurred to me that the extra bit of discomfort my mother was suffering was something I *could* stop.

The whole point of my flying a thousand miles to stay with my mother in the hospital was to try to provide some comfort during what turned out to be her final days. I'd gotten a portable player with her favorite Dead Can Dance and The Incredible String Band CDs. I'd read to her from *To Kill a Mockingbird*, her favorite book. But the one thing I could have really done to make things better was the one thing I was too stupid to do.

A few hours later, the morning nurse would come in and declare, "Well, if it were my mother, *I'd* have called someone in to clean her up!"

And then, shamefaced and embarrassed, I'd go home to try to sleep.

And then my mother would die while I was gone. While nobody was looking. While nobody was there to hold her hand.

The nurse's words would take root in my memory and grow, tainting every other memory they touched. They were loud in my head when I swallowed the bottle of tranquilizers. And they never went away even after the few post-hospital therapy sessions my insurance grudgingly covered. They would never, ever go away, condemnation and proof that I had failed my mom.

"Vicky." My mother sat up in bed and was giving me a stern look.

My heart jumped when I realized that she saw me. I felt pierced by her amber eyes. "Yes?"

"The blood was a little uncomfortable, yes. But my intestines were being torn apart by microbes and cancer. My kidneys were rotting inside my body. A little itch on my neck just didn't matter, you know? Stop beating yourself up over it. That's an order, okay?"

"Yes, ma'am."

She beckoned me closer and held out her bone-thin arms for a hug. The invisible wall didn't block me this time. I sat down on the bed beside her and held her close. As I breathed in the familiar scents of her perfume and hair spray, I was overwhelmed at the enormity of what I'd lost when she died, and I began to weep.

"I'm so sorry you died alone," I sobbed. "I'm so, so sorry. I wanted to be there for you."

"But you were!" My mother gently pushed me back and wiped the tears off my face with her thumbs like she had when I was little. "I heard the music, I heard you read. I knew you were there. I wasn't even conscious when I died. It was like slipping from sleep into…more sleep. It wasn't scary. You didn't fail me."

She turned to the hospital tray beside her bed and picked up three small brown nuts beside her insulated plastic water jug.

"Hold out your hand," she said.

I did as she asked, and she dropped the nuts onto my palm.

"What are these?"

"Hazelnuts," she replied. "For wisdom, healing, and maybe a little inspiration for those books of yours."

"Thank you." I tucked them into the left front pocket of my jeans.

"Have a happy Halloween." My mother gave me a gentle push, and I tumbled backward off the bed into darkness.

I came to in the bed in my hotel room. The room was dark except for a head-splitting band of light under the blackout curtain. My head ached, and my mouth felt fuzzy. I still wore my convention clothes. Heather was snoring away in the other bed.

"Ugh." I moaned like a zombie.

"Oh, thank goodness you're awake!" Elaine said. I heard her get up from the desk chair and walk to the bed. "You need to drink water; here's an Aquafina."

I took a tentative sip from the bottle she stuck close to my face. The water was cool and delicious, so I took a longer draw.

"We looked all over for you," Elaine said. "Nicole found you in the convention center basement—how you got down there, we'll never know! She says you were hugging a steam pipe. You're lucky you didn't get burned!"

"Lucky. Yeah. I gotta go pee."

"Let me help you—"

"Nah, I got this."

I rolled out of the bed and staggered toward the toilet.

Heather's sleep-frowsy head rose from the sheets.

"Hey, I saved the Great Pumpkin," she slurred at me.

"Good job!" I locked the bathroom door behind me in case Elaine decided I needed assistance. To be fair, she was probably panicking that I was going to sue her and the convention for feeding me illicit drugs. I went to the toilet and unzipped my glitter-smeared jeans and heard something fall out of my back pocket onto the floor.

It was a package of Lik-a-Stik Yummy Mummies.

I pulled my jeans back up and reached into my left front pocket. My finger encountered something round and hard: the three hazelnuts. I took them out and stared at them for several minutes, rolling them around on my palm with the tip of my finger. One for healing, one for wisdom, and one for inspiration. One for me, one for Mom, and one for Joe. One for my past, one for my present, and one for my future.

Elaine rapped gently on the door. "Are you okay in there?"

"Yes, I'm fine," I replied.

And realized that, for a change, I actually was.

Cosmic Cola

Millie leaned her forehead against the back window of her stepfather's new Toyota van, morosely watching the weather-beaten, navy-on-white "Welcome to Marsh Landing!" sign approach and recede. Welcome to what? There was little but some bone-white dunes and shuttered, peeling bait shacks so far. Nothing she'd learned about the isolated coastal town in her school's library made her feel any better about moving here. Population: 20,000. Primary export: fish and Cosmic Cola. Total Dullsville. It was probably one of those stuffy communities that forbade trick-or-treat at Halloween. Marsh Middle School was barely half the size of her old school and didn't have any Girl Scouts troops she could join. It didn't even have an orchestra. She'd only just started playing violin and already she was going to have to quit, probably.

Quitters never got anywhere in life. That's what her grandfather Ernest always used to tell her anyhow, before he had a stroke and quit living. In the months before he died, he'd argue about physics when he was alone in his room, as if the empty walls were his audience. She could play her violin in her room and pretend she had an audience, she supposed, but her bedroom walls wouldn't tell her if she dropped a note, or if her bowing was scratchy, or if her phrasing was awkward. So even if she kept going on her own, she wasn't sure she'd get anywhere anyway.

If she was honest with herself, giving up violin didn't bother her nearly as much as the notion of giving up Halloween. It was her favorite holiday, even better than Christmas, though she could never say that out loud. Her mom would say it wasn't *ladylike* to prefer Halloween over Jesus' birthday. And her love for it wasn't just because of trick-or-treating. It was the one night when all the things she dreamed of seemed like they could actually become real. The one night when she didn't have to always be nice and demure and could be something besides a girl from a little town in a flyover state. She could be a ghost. A witch. A werewolf. Something mythical, something to be feared and respected. Running down the street in her costume, she could close her eyes in the frosty fall air and just for a moment imagine that plastic teeth and waxy paints were enamel and skin, and she could go anywhere at all that she wanted on her own. What was Christmas compared to the chilly frisson of *becoming*?

"Gimme!" On the middle seat, her little half-brother Travis reached for his twin sister's Cabbage Patch doll.

"Nooo!" Tiffany hugged the doll to her chest and turned away from her brother's grabby hands. "Mooom!"

"Leave your sister's toys alone." Their mother's tone was one of utter exhaustion. Was exhaustion an emotion, or the lack of it? Millie wasn't sure. "Play with your Star Wars figures."

"Fifty," Millie announced.

"What?" Her mother turned in her seat and squinted at her tiredly.

"That's the fiftieth time you've said those exact words on this trip."

Her mother's lips twitched into a half-smile. "You counted?"

"I did." Millie couldn't keep the satisfaction out of her voice. She was *very* good at counting. Last year she'd won a $50 gift certificate in a contest at Harmon's Grocery to guess how many jellybeans were in a big jar, and was a little sad afterward when she found out that since she won once she couldn't compete again. She'd missed the count by 248, and was sure she could have done even better the next time.

Her stepfather cleared his throat, obviously annoyed. "Doesn't Madame Curie have a book to read?"

Her mother shot him a dirty look but didn't say anything. Millie felt her face grow hot. Her stepfather had started calling her "Madame Curie" after she won the school science fair with her homemade electrolysis set. And at first it had seemed like a nice thing, as if after five years of being her stepfather he was starting to like her a little bit and to be proud of her accomplishments, like he was proud of Tiffany and Travis. After all, Marie Curie was the only person in history to win Nobel Prizes in two different sciences! So calling her Madame Curie couldn't really be a bad thing, could it? But the way he started saying it after the first couple of times…it tasted like a razor blade inside a Tootsie Roll. But if she said anything, he'd just accuse her of not being able to take a compliment. Of not having a sense of humor. Of being a brat.

"I *had* a book to read," she said, trying to keep her voice steady, "and I read it."

"Then you should have brought more." His tone was hard as the pavement beneath his van's black tires.

"I brought *four*. And I read them all." Her heart was beating so fast her vision was starting to twitch.

The twins had gone silent in the seat in front of her, like nest-bound fledglings beneath the shadow of a hawk.

"You did *not* read four books in the past six hours." He stared at her in the rearview mirror, his gaze as steady as any raptor's.

"Did, too." She grabbed her library book sale copies of *Bunnicula, Superfudge, Blubber,* and *From the Mixed-Up Files of Mrs. Basil E. Frankweiler* and held them up so he could see them. "I read them cover to cover. Ask me about them. Ask me *anything.*"

She wasn't lying, and she knew that he hadn't enough of a clue about any of the books to even begin to question her about them. He'd made it clear he considered them to be kids' books, *girl* books, and he was a man. A man with a brand-new van and a fancy important job. Nothing in the books could interest him, so why bother? The idea of seeking a subject to discuss with his stepdaughter was so far from his orbit it could take him millennia to discover it.

"If you were so busy reading back there, how could you possibly know what your mother said to the twins?" There was a talon of warning in his tone: she had better stop challenging him, or else.

Or else what? she wondered bitterly. *Or else you'll take me away from everything I care about and drop me in some dumpy awful town that probably stinks of fish? Just because you got a job at some stupid soft drink company?*

Why couldn't he have gone away to work and left them where they were? Other dads did that to keep from uprooting their families. But her half-siblings weren't in school yet, so she was the only one being uprooted. Her real father had brought her mother to Greensburg so they could be closer to his father, and Mom hadn't liked it there since Grandpa Ernest died. She said that seeing his old room every day made her feel sad. And Millie wanted her mom to be happy. She *did*. But…ugh.

"I can count and read at the same time," she replied defiantly.

"Hey, look, it's our street," her mother exclaimed in the loud, overly cheery tone she used when she was trying to distract her stepfather.

"Craftsman Lane!" She patted his hand on the steering wheel. "This is so exciting, isn't it honey? Our first real house together!"

Millie glared down at her lap, feeling a spike of irritation at her mom's comment. The old house had been real enough, but Millie's father bought it before he died, and so it wasn't *their* house. But now they could move someplace new and pretend that Millie's real father had never even existed. It wasn't fair.

"Oh, what a lovely hibiscus!" her mother said.

Millie finally looked out the window and blinked in surprise. They had gone from dunes and bait shacks to a proper town with tree-shaded neighborhood streets. Teen boys were kicking a soccer ball around on a well-kept corner field. This place didn't look *too* bad, she had to admit. Maybe there would be some kids her age in the neighborhood? She hadn't had a lot of friends at her old school. She and Chrissy Romano were pretty tight, at least until Chrissy started having eyes for Mike Walhgren. Millie walked to school with Jeff Laramie for years and had thought of him as a friend until he joined Little League and decided he was too cool to hang out with girls. Sixth grade was confusing; everybody wanted to be with the boys and nobody wanted to spend time with Millie.

So, maybe seventh grade would be better? Maybe meeting new kids would be the one good thing about having to leave everything she knew behind?

Her stepfather slowed in front of a three-story white Victorian with a wraparound porch. "And here's our new home!"

Millie couldn't take her eyes off the amazing porch. It had steps wide enough for pumpkins on each side, and a railing that was begging to be decorated. "That's the perfect Halloween porch!"

"Aren't you getting a little old for Halloween?" her stepfather said.

"Not yet," Millie suddenly felt anxious. She couldn't tell from his tone if he was being serious.

"I think you are." He pulled the van into the driveway and parked. "I think you're getting much too old for things like Halloween and trick-or-treating."

"You said *teenagers* are too old. I'm not a teenager. Not until next April." She turned to her mother, her stomach churning. She *couldn't* be too old for Halloween. Not yet. "You said I could still trick-or-treat this year."

"Oh, honey, that's a whole three months away," her mother said. "Let's go in and see our new home!"

The house was fine. Millie's new room got too much sun in the mornings, but as her mother pointed out, at least she wasn't running late for school any more. Her stepfather was frequently gone on Cosmic Cola business—he bought her mother a Honda Civic so they wouldn't have to share his van—and frankly his absence was a relief. And Marsh Middle School was fine, too, at least as far as her classes went.

The kids were weird, though. She was used to the cliques at Wendover: orchestra kids, theatre kids, rich kids, poor kids. Pretty kids from wealthy families who were good at sports were at the top, and the special ed kids and the immigrant kids from poor families were at the bottom. It wasn't fair but it made sense. But at Marsh, it was mostly about whose families had been around the longest. Even the kid with crooked, discolored teeth and a limp got to sit with the popular kids at lunch because he was a real Marsh. So did the kid with the threadbare clothes. Sure, they had a hierarchy within their hierarchy, but nobody who was "new blood" got let into that club no matter how cool they were. And apparently you could still be new blood even if your family had lived in the town for several generations…but meanwhile some of the other kids were considered old blood even though they'd moved to town just a few years before. The situation wasn't any fairer than at Wendover, and Millie couldn't quite make sense of it, not entirely.

The old blood kids were actually friendlier to Millie than they were to some of the new blood kids they'd grown up with, simply because when the teachers introduced her, they made sure to mention that her father was the new Vice President of Operations for Cosmic Cola. Millie never would have guessed that being the daughter of an executive at the soda company would be such a big deal. It was nearly as good as being a featured soloist in the choir! She didn't make new friends, not like Chrissy had been, anyway, but she always had a place to sit at lunch and people to talk to and nobody picked on her.

Once she realized the social advantage she had, she could never let on that she didn't even *like* Cosmic Cola. It was sickly sweet, and it had an unpleasant licorice aftertaste. And the bubbles were too harsh and made her sneeze. Everybody in town seemed to drink gallons of the stuff. Whenever someone offered her a bottle, she'd politely pretend to sip it and then pour it out first chance she got.

Late summer cooled to fall, and at the end of September the janitors festooned the school in black-and-orange streamers and grinning paper Jack-o-Lanterns, black cats, and green-faced witches. Millie was thrilled! Marsh Middle School was far more keen on Halloween than her old school was. And not only did the town have an official trick-or-treat planned from 6pm to 8pm on Halloween, they had special Devil's Night parties planned for older kids and teens on the days leading up to Halloween to prevent pranks and other mischief in town.

The biggest Devil's Night party—or at least the most *important* party as far as her classmates were concerned—was the Cosmic Cola Party at Marsh Mansion up on the cliff above the ocean. None of the Marsh family lived there anymore; old Jeremiah Marsh had donated it to the soda company for charity events and executive retreats. They'd get to ride in a chartered bus up the winding road to the mansion, and at the party they'd dance and drink Cosmic Cola and eat pizza and play games. All that, on the face of it, didn't seem so impressive to Millie, but the old blood kids all talked about how their parents had said that the company was bringing in a super-secret special guest to play at the party. Some said it might be Aerosmith…others claimed it was Duran Duran or even Michael Jackson.

Millie's mother said she was far too young to go to a rock concert, so to think that she might be able to see someone as famous as Michael Jackson…that was *most* impressive. And even better, because the party ran so late, all the kids who attended would be excused from class the next day.

The catch was that only thirty kids from Marsh Middle School could attend the party, and they'd be chosen in a special lottery in mid-October. Everyone got one ticket, but students could earn extra tickets by making As, volunteering to help out around the school, and other such things. By October 7th, she'd earned seven lottery tickets thanks to her good grades in math, English and history and a couple afternoons picking up trash. Seven was more than most kids, but she guessed that there were probably 900 tickets total for the 300 kids in the school, which meant that her efforts had earned her only a fraction of a percent of a chance.

And then she had a worrisome thought.

"Papa, I was wondering about something," she said that night at dinner. Her mother and stepfather preferred that she called him Papa, rather than Steve or Mr. Gibbs. Calling him that almost didn't seem unnatural anymore.

"Yes?" He took a bite of meatloaf. "What is it?"

"The Cosmic Cola party…you work for the company. I won't be excluded from the lottery, will I?"

"No, not at all," he replied cheerfully. "You've got as much of a chance as any other kid. Better, I expect, since you got all those extra tickets."

Her mother suddenly looked anxious. "You shouldn't get your hopes up, dear. So few kids get picked. But don't worry; there are plenty of other parties that evening. There'll be a sock hop party at DiLouie's Pizza; that sounds like fun, don't you think?"

Millie shrugged and ate her mashed potatoes. The pizza parlor wouldn't have Michael Jackson except on the jukebox.

Her stepfather fixed a sharp gaze on her mother. "But if she *is* chosen, it's an honor to go."

He turned back to Millie and smiled. "Cosmic Cola is putting a lot of effort and money into this party for you kids. If you're chosen, you'll be representing our whole family, so you need to be on your best behavior. Can I count on you?"

His words made Millie feel uneasy; how could a party for a bunch of middle schoolers really be such a big deal? But she knew what he wanted to hear. "Yes, sir. You can count on me."

She looked at her mother; Mrs. Gibbs' face had gone white and she was staring down at her half-eaten plate. Her expression was carefully blank but her eyes shimmered as if she was holding back tears. It was then that Millie realized her mother was not happy, and something was happening here that Millie could but dimly grasp. She wanted to go around the table to give her mother a hug, but she knew that would break some unwritten, unspoken rule; her mother would be embarrassed and her stepfather would be angry, but neither adult would tell her what was wrong. Millie felt as though she were a boat adrift far from shore beneath storm-gathering skies.

The school's portly vice principal reached into the clear plastic raffle tumbler full of names on folded white notecards. He picked one out and opened it with a theatrical flourish.

"Millie Flynn," he announced into his microphone.

Millie sat in shock on the wooden gymnasium bleacher at hearing her name called. The girl beside her started shrieking in excitement and shaking her shoulder, and soon Millie was whooping and high-fiving the other kids near her who'd been chosen for the party, too.

After the school assembly was over, Millie had study hall, and her excitement faded into curiosity. She and 21 other new blood kids and eight old blood kids had been picked. Why had so few of the old blood kids been chosen? The kid with the limp and the crooked, discolored teeth was one of them. She still wasn't sure what his name was. But, she reasoned, the old blood kids hadn't tried very hard. They hadn't been the ones volunteering for chores to earn extra tickets. They hadn't studied late trying to earn straight As. They weren't the ones who had to prove they belonged in Marsh Landing.

When she got home and told her parents the news, her stepfather seemed pleased and her mother smiled and congratulated her. Millie could see something like panic behind her eyes. That night after dinner, her father went to his Cosmic Cola bowling league, and her mother put the twins to bed.

As Millie was helping her mother wash and dry the dishes, her mother asked, "Have you thought about the costume you'll wear to the party?"

Millie considered. "A little. I liked being a witch last year, but my dress and stockings are too small now."

Her mother smiled, her eyes still dark with worry. "You've shot up like a weed this past year. You're nearly as tall as I am, now."

"Maybe I could be a werewolf this year? I saw a cool mask in the window of the costume shop."

"I had an idea," her mother said, looking around as if she was making sure that her stepfather wasn't still in the house. "Why don't you go as a pirate queen?"

Millie blinked. "A pirate queen?"

"They probably didn't tell you this in school, but a lot of women were very fierce pirates back in the day. Jacquotte Delahaye was a Caribbean pirate in the 1600s. They called her 'Back from the Dead Red' after she faked her own death to escape the British Navy. She became a pirate after her father died and eventually she became a master swordswoman and commanded a fleet of hundreds of pirates. She ruled over her own island. Ruling an island makes you a proper queen, don't you think?"

"Whoa," Millie said. Already in her mind she was swashbuckling on a beach, protecting a loot-laden chest from scowling English redcoats in pompous white wigs. "Yeah, for sure!"

Her mother dried the last dish and put it away in the cupboard. Her hand shook just a little as she set it down. "I was out shopping at the thrift store the other day, and I found some things in your size that I think would make a good pirate costume. Would you like to see them?"

"Ooh, yes!" Millie clapped her hands.

Her mother led her down into her sewing room in the finished basement.

"I found this." Her mother reached into a white plastic shopping bag and pulled out a gorgeous wig of long, thickly ringleted red hair. It looked like something from a fancy salon and not a cheap dime store Halloween wig.

"It's so pretty!" Millie breathed.

Her mother looked pleased, but the fearful shadows hadn't left her eyes. "Well, Back From the Dead Red needs proper red hair!" She pulled out another shopping bag and laid out a rakish blue scarf, a blowsy white shirt with laces instead of buttons, a black leatherette vest, tan pants, a thick black belt, black knee-high boots, and a bunch of golden bangles. And a real genuine brass compass! It was so much nicer than the ones they'd learned to read in Girl Scouts, and it looked like something a real pirate would own.

Millie threw her arms around her mother's neck. "This is great! Thank you sooo much!"

Trembling, her mother returned the hug, rubbing Millie's back in gentle circles. "It's your last Halloween, and you're going to a very important party, so I wanted you to feel proud of your costume."

Millie hugged her mother more tightly. "You're the best."

Her mother began to cry and shake.

Millie pulled back and gazed at her mother, worried. "What's the matter, Mom?"

"Nothing, nothing." Her mother quickly wiped her red eyes and smiled widely. Unconvincingly. "I…you're just growing up so quickly. It makes me sad sometimes."

Her mother glanced at the compass lying beside the costume on the sewing table. "You remember how to use a compass, don't you?"

"Oh, yes, absolutely. It was my favorite part of camp craft!" That was a little lie; really Millie had liked building fires best, but she knew that didn't sound ladylike.

Her mother was still blinking back tears. "I think having a compass is a good idea in case they take you out someplace and you get separated from the rest of the kids. It's easy to get lost in an unfamiliar town, you know?"

Millie didn't, but she nodded anyway.

"Marsh Mansion is due southeast of here. If you had to get back here on your own, go north on Oceanside Highway and follow it to 6th Street, go left, and then take a left on Craftsman Lane. And you'll find us!"

That sounded like a whole lot of walking. "If I got lost, couldn't I just find a payphone and call you?"

"Oh, honey, that's a smart idea but not on Devil's Night," her mother replied quickly. "Your stepfather's concerned about prank callers and he's planning to leave the phone off the hook. So if something happens, just try to get back here, okay? I'll stay up waiting for you; just knock quietly and I'll know it's you. If it's late, we don't want to wake the twins or your stepfather. He hasn't been sleeping well and you know what a terrible mood he gets in when something wakes him suddenly."

Millie did. "Okay, I'll just come back and knock quietly if something happens."

"But nothing will! This is all just for contingency's sake. I'm sure you'll have a wonderful time."

"Okay."

A flash of remembering crossed her mother's face. "Oh! And I forgot the most important part of your costume." She went to the closet and retrieved a long white cardboard box. Inside was a cutlass with a tarnished brass basket guard in a worn leather scabbard. When she pulled the blade out a few inches, it gleamed steely and cold.

Millie could barely believe her eyes. "Whoa, is that a real sword?"

"It's a costume sword, but it's still pretty sharp, so don't go waving it around. Can you believe that this was actually cheaper at the thrift store than a plastic pirate's cutlass at the toy shop? Prices these days! Anyhow, this looks better with your costume, and you're mature enough to leave it sheathed so nobody knows it's dangerous, aren't you?"

Millie nodded vigorously. Her own real sword! "I'll just tell people it's wooden."

Her mother smiled again, looking relieved. "Good girl. I have one more thing."

From the pocket of her apron, she pulled out a silvery flask, the kind Old West gamblers and gangsters put liquor in. "I know you don't really like Cosmic Cola, and that's practically the only thing they'll be serving at the party. This way, you can take something else to drink. Just, try not to let anybody see you with it, or they might think you have something you shouldn't. And that would have… consequences." She paused, rubbing her throat lightly. "Don't tell your stepfather about the flask. Or the sword. He wouldn't approve."

"I won't." Inside, Millie glowed with pleasure at her mother taking her into such confidence. Her own sword *and* a flask? This wasn't just the kind of cool boy stuff she'd previously been forbidden from on the grounds it wasn't ladylike; this was actual grown-up stuff! She was treating Millie like she was an adult! *Finally*!

Her mother smiled. "Well, it's an hour until your bedtime…want to go outside and carve a pumpkin or two?"

"Ooh, yes!" This was going to be the best Halloween *ever*!

On Devil's Night, Millie's stepfather had some kind of meeting he had to go to, so he wasn't around when her mother helped her get dressed in her pirate costume for the party.

"There." Her mother adjusted the red wig, which was much heavier than Millie had expected, as was the lemonade-filled flask in the inside pocket of her vest. Even the brass compass rested more heavily than she expected in her right hip pocket. And the brass-hilted sword hanging against her left hip—Millie had spray-painted it in brown Rustoleum so it looked a little less suspiciously real—was heaviest of all. "Perfect. Turn around and take a look."

Millie did. The wig and her mother's makeup job to give her a proper Caribbean tan made her look much older, but more important, she looked like a real pirate!

"This is so cool! Thank you!" She hugged her mom.

Her mom hugged her back tightly. "You know I love you, right?"

"Of course," Millie mumbled into her mom's shoulder.

"I love you bunches and bunches. I know that, sometimes, I do things that don't seem fair, and I'm sorry about that. I just can't change how some things are. Steve and I have to worry about what's best for the twins, and…well, let's get you to the party."

By the time Millie's mother dropped her off at the school stadium parking lot, the 29 other kids were clustered under a tall light, giggling and horsing around as they waited for the Cosmic Cola chartered bus to pick them up. Fifteen boys, and fifteen girls. Seven of the girls were dressed up as different kinds of witches; three were fairy princesses, three were black cats, and one was dressed as Princess Leia. The boys had a more diverse set of costumes; Millie figured it was because they had more movie characters to pick from. There was a Han Solo, an Indiana Jones, a cop, two Karate Kids, a Captain Kirk, three Ghostbusters, a Rocky Balboa, a Batman, a Superman, a solider, a masked slasher…and a pirate captain, who she was dismayed to realize was the old blood kid with the limp and crooked teeth. It made her feel weird that they'd chosen similar costumes. She felt her cheeks heat with embarrassment when he looked up at her and grinned and waved.

The Cosmic Cola bus rolled up, and a pretty woman in a mini-skirted black-tie magician's costume stepped out onto the pavement. The boys whispered she was dressed like a character named Zatanna from the comics, and once again Millie was annoyed that her parents had forbidden comic books, because she hated knowing less than the other kids.

"Hey, kids!" Zatanna beamed at them all. "Are you ready for the party?"

The crowd exploded in "Yeah!" and "Woo!"

"Well, everybody get on! Your party awaits!"

Millie was swept up in the boiling wave of seventh graders and shoved onto the bus. She stumbled into a row and plopped down on the plush red velvet window seat…and her heart dropped when the weird kid sat down beside her.

"Hey." He extended his hand. "My name's Hubert."

She awkwardly took his hand and shook it. "I'm Millie."

"Yes, I know. Your father's the new executive. He must be so proud that you got chosen."

Millie squirmed in her seat; Hubert was looking at her so intently, and…it was all just so weird. "Yeah, I mean, I guess."

"*My* father's *super* proud." Hubert gave her a snaggle-toothed smile. "He was always so disappointed that I was born with my legs messed up, and the doctors couldn't really fix them, but now I get to do something really good for the whole family tonight."

"Why is this party such a big deal?"

"Well, it's the thirty year, and…" He paused, wincing a little, seeming to realize that maybe he'd said something he shouldn't. "Well, it's just going to be something special. You'll see."

Zatanna went up and down the aisle with a narrow serving cart laden with apple cider donuts, popcorn balls, bags of chips, frosted Halloween cookies, and of course cans of Cosmic Cola.

"They'll have pizza at the party, too." Hubert grabbed double-fistfuls of donuts. "You want something?"

"No, thank you; I'm saving room for pizza." Feeling unsettled, Millie turned away to watch the Marsh Landing Lighthouse and the rest of the dark landscape pass outside the bus windows.

🦇

They reached Marsh Mansion just before 9pm. It was a huge old place, built on a low cliff above the ocean, all covered in Victorian gingerbread and wrought iron balconies and railings.

Zatanna and the bus driver—a gruff, heavyset man who'd been silent the entire trip—ushered them all off the bus and into the mansion's vaulted foyer.

"Last year, we had the party in the second-floor ballroom, but there was a leak and some of the ceiling came down last week," Zatanna said brightly. "So this year, the party is in the downstairs grotto."

She opened up a pair of double doors at the side of the foyer that revealed wide stone steps with a wrought iron wall railing that coiled downward. The bass line of Michael Jackson's "Thriller" boomed faintly from below. "Everybody, follow me!"

The kids all jostled down the stairs. Millie gripped the iron railing, partly to avoid getting knocked over, but partly to still her nerves, which had been jangling ever since Hubert's comment. She felt badly for judging the boy on his looks, but it wasn't just his looks that made her recoil, and her instincts told her that anything he liked, she should be wary of. But that was silly; everyone said this party was a huge honor. Everyone. Her stepfather, her mother, the vice principal, the other kids. It wasn't possible that everyone could be wrong.

The railing was very cold, and slick from condensation. The air grew colder and damper and the music got louder as they went down, down at least three stories into the earth. She was glad for the cover of her vest. The widely spiraling stairs were at first lit with electric lights, but those changed to guttering, Medieval-looking torches in iron sconces.

"Mind the open flames!" Zatanna called up over the music. "Don't get burned!"

Just as the music switched to Duran Duran's "Hungry Like The Wolf," the stairs opened up into a big natural cave whose walls were strung with white-and-orange string lights. Along the left side was a big buffet line with a half-dozen pizzas from DiLouie's in white cardboard boxes and few steel banquet serving bins atop flickering Sterno cans. At the end of the long table beyond the food were plastic tubs of different flavors of Cosmic Colas on ice. There wasn't even any water. Millie was glad she brought her flask.

On the right side of the cave were some big heavy steel barn doors which had either corroded or were painted a rust brown. A bit of water puddled beneath them, and Millie wondered where they led.

The side of the cave directly opposite the stairs held a raised stage with a few big speakers and some sound equipment but no instruments. A DJ in a black turtleneck and jeans and a pair of huge headphones sat at a sound panel with a couple of turntables and reel-to-reel deck beside the stage. He gave her a little wave when he noticed her staring at him, and that made her flush with embarrassment and look away. And when she looked away, she noticed four other men—chaperones? security guards?—standing quietly in alcoves carved into the limestone walls. They were also dressed in black, and at first glance she thought they were statues or decorative dummies, but then one scratched his nose.

"Dig in, kids!" Zatanna shouted over the booming music. "Our very special musical guest will be out in a little while!"

The seventh graders swarmed to the food line, chattering and pogoing with excitement as they flopped pizza onto paper plates with greasy fingers. The other kids had gotten increasingly rambunctious as they'd drunk more soda and eaten more sweets, and the louder they all got, the more Millie lost her appetite and wished she could be someplace that wasn't so noisy. And that frustrated her. She was finally someplace cool with the cool kids; why couldn't she enjoy it? Why couldn't she just join in like everybody else?

Was this what getting old was like? To feel isolated in the midst of a huge crowd and want to be someplace quiet? To feel oppressed rather than privileged to be in the middle of something everybody said was cool?

The DJ cued up Madonna's "Holiday" and a bunch of the kids started dancing, Cosmic Cola cans sloshing in their hands.

"You should get some pizza!" Hubert yelled at her elbow.

She turned toward him, startled. His eyes were glassy, and he had an enormous grin on his sweaty, flushed face. He gripped what had to be his third or fourth Cosmic Cola of the evening.

"I will," she yelled back. "In a minute or two!"

"Okay," he replied. "I'm not trying to boss you. It's just you should enjoy yourself! You earned it!"

I should, she thought. *I should stop being a stick in the mud and get some pizza, at least.*

Just as she made her way to the back of the buffet line, she saw a group of men and women in strange hooded robes come down the stairs in single file. Startled kids stopped dancing and let them pass as they made their way to the stage. When the last hooded figure—the 13th—had emerged from the stairway, two of the silent men in black suits pulled an iron gate Millie hadn't noticed over the entry to the stairs and chained it shut. The girl's stomach dropped and she lost any and all interest in pizza.

The DJ stopped the music and turned on the stage lights. Zatanna stepped up and approached the microphone.

"And here's our special musical guests tonight, direct from Innsmouth," she announced. "The Esoteric Order of Dagon Choir! Let's all give them a hand!"

Some of the new blood kids started golf-clapping uncertainly, but Hubert and the other old blood kids started cheering and whistling and stomping their feet and chanting like they were at a football game: *"FAA-ther DAA-gon! FAA-ther DAA-gon!"*

Millie blinked, feeling profoundly confused and unsettled. This didn't make any sense. Was Father Dagon the lead singer? Or was it the name of a song? What was going on here?

Zatanna hopped offstage. The leader of the group pushed his hood back and stepped regally to the microphone. The old, thin, white-bearded man scanned the crowd of kids. He wore a strange golden crown that was all high, asymmetrical spires in front with some coralline flourishes around the headband. It both looked like something someone found at the bottom of the sea and something she'd expect to see floating in outer space.

"You are the Chosen," he intoned into the microphone. "You are the Promised. You are the Honored. Tonight you ascend as you descend, and the gift of your lives ensures that Father Dagon smiles kindly upon your families and communities for the next generation. Those of you whose families are outsiders, rejoice! From this night forward, your sacrifice ensures that your bloodlines flow with ours. Your kin will be joined with the host, and you will all be profoundly blessed."

Millie felt her heart flutter in her chest and she took a step back, bumping into Hubert. The gift of their lives? *Sacrifice?*

"Father Dagon, take me first!" Hubert screamed behind her.

Millie frantically looked around for some other exit, or a place to hide, but there was none. Just the heavy metal barn doors that led someplace dark and watery, and the chained gate to the stairs.

The man with the crown took a deep breath, as did the twelve choir members behind him, and they began to sing. It was loud, like opera, but there was no melody and the voices of the chorus ground against each other like glass in disharmony. Millie's whole body broke out in goosebumps and her heart pounded in her chest and she plugged her fingers in her ears, but there was no getting away from this strange, horrible, atonal music, no way to keep it from pounding into her skull like hurricane waves smashing against the beach, no way to keep from feeling like someone was reaching inside her skull and twisting her brains until up was down and down was up, and it was all so terrible that she just wanted to laugh and laugh and never stop….

And the other children around her were laughing, laughing 'til they shrieked, laughing 'til they vomited up pizza and sweets and Cosmic Cola. The still-sane part of Millie's mind noticed that Zatanna and the men had gotten out hard-shelled ear muffs like her stepfather wore when he went to the gun range. And they just stood there on the margins, wearing their ear protection, impassively watching and waiting…for what?

Hubert finished puking behind her and gasped, "It's happening! It's happening! Praise Father Dagon, I am Becoming!"

She turned. The boy's whole head was swelling up like a grotesque balloon, his eyes bulging, his mouth widening impossibly. His back and shoulders hunched spasmodically, and she heard the crack of breaking bone. He yawned, making a terrible retching sound, and Millie watched in horror as his crooked white incisors, bicuspids and molars popped bloodily from his jaw, jumping free like popcorn kernels, only to be followed by the sharp grey irregular jags of brand-new teeth erupting through his raw gums, teeth like a shark's or a barracuda's. His eyes had bulged so much she was sure they'd pop right out of his head, the whites turning black, his blue irises turning a mottled golden like a frog's.

His skin split over his swollen flesh and he started furiously scratching himself with newly-clawed paws, tearing his clothing and pale skin away to reveal mottled, moist scales beneath. He threw the last rags of his captain's costume aside and crouched naked on muscular frog's legs, croaking hoarsely at her.

The awful sight of Hubert's transformation sent adrenaline surging through Millie's blood, and that broke the spell of the eldritch choir. She stepped away from the hopping abomination that Hubert had become and looked all around her, again seeking escape when she knew there was none. All the other kids were turning into monstrous fish-frogs. Everybody changing into something mythical and terrifying. Everyone but her.

The sane, calm part of her mind made note that while the dark part of her mind had long dreamed of being able to become something feared and respected, something that could send all the kids who'd ever bullied her and all the adults who'd ever belittled her screaming for the safety of locked doors…she most certainly did not want to become one of these god-awful things. They *stank*. Sweet lord, they stank like fish and vomit and blood. And one look in their bulging eyes and she just knew that they weren't in control of their own minds. They were slaves to Father Dagon.

If Millie ever became a monster, she wanted it to be on her own terms.

"Children, rejoice!" The leader of the choir shouted over the abominable song. "You are remade in your Father's image, and now you shall meet him!"

Two of the men from the alcoves pulled open the huge metal barn doors, and suddenly the grotto was filled with the smell of seawater and the sound of crashing surf. Immediately, the gibbering, baying, croaking fish-frogs swarmed toward the water, and Millie was carried along with them. She managed to take a deep breath right before they all plunged into the dark, surging waves.

Immediately, she lost her gorgeous red wig amongst the thrashing, splashing limbs. Millie had never been a fast swimmer, but she had always been a strong one. It was hard to swim in her boots and poofy-sleeved shirt, hard to keep her head above water with the brass sword weighing her down in the croaking throng surging out to sea, but she did it.

The throng thinned, and Millie distantly glimpsed the sweeping spotlight in the lighthouse, which she remembered the bus passing. That way was town, and her parents' house. Safety.

She started to awkwardly breast-stroke toward the lighthouse, but something grabbed her. Hubert's awful croaking face loomed beside hers, his bulging eyes gleaming with mindless hunger.

Millie shrieked and scrabbled her pirate's cutlass out of its scabbard and jabbed it at him. She felt the blade sink into something soft. Hubert let out an inhuman barking cry and released her. She gave the sword another shove and let it go, too, splashing away as fast as she could.

He didn't follow.

Millie staggered to shore on the rocky beach a few hundred yards north of the mansion. Her arms and legs were numb with cold. She was so exhausted she wanted to lie down and sleep, but she knew she couldn't. The people from the mansion could find her here, and she wasn't convinced that some of the fish-frogs wouldn't track her down. Besides, she'd learned about hypothermia in Girl Scouts, and if she didn't keep moving she might get so cold she'd die. She sat down on a rock to pour the seawater out of her boots and wring out her socks as best she could. Her feet were wrinkled from her swim, and she had no doubt they'd be covered in the worst blisters she'd ever had by the time she got home.

The compass had stayed in her back pocket, and when she pulled it out, she was surprised to find that it had been waterproofed and still worked fine. She put her damp socks and boots back on and kept going down the beach, hoping that the rocky cliffs would end soon so she could get back onto the highway like her mother had told her.

"Like my mother told me," she repeated aloud to herself.

The sudden shock of realization made her stop and stand very still, shivering. Her mother had known this was going to happen. Maybe not *exactly* what had happened, but she knew *something* bad would happen. Why had she sent her to the party if she knew? Had her own mother betrayed her? Millie felt a new surge of terror and anger. If her mother was in on this, could she still go home?

But no. She shook her head, scolding herself. Her mom loved her. She *did*. She'd given Millie a real sword! And a flask so she wouldn't have to drink the hateful Cosmic Cola. She'd given her the tools she needed to escape. Millie couldn't understand why her mom would send her into the mouth of horror when her entire life she'd kept Millie away from anything and everything that seemed even slightly dangerous. But, she had…and Millie figured her mother had some explaining to do. At *least*.

Further, even if Millie did want to run away, where could she go? She didn't know how to contact any of her other relatives, and she didn't have any money for a bus or even for a pay phone. Millie had seen enough thrillers to suspect a conspiracy, and she didn't know who could be trusted. If she couldn't trust her own mom, she certainly couldn't trust neighbors or teachers she'd only known for a few months, could she? There wasn't much choice except to go home.

Shivering in the fitful wind, Millie plodded along the dark beach, eyes downcast, until she smelled burning gasoline and glimpsed the flicker of flames in her peripheral vision. She looked up. The Cosmic Cola bus had crashed over the guardrail onto its side and was burning. The whole thing was engulfed. Two firetrucks were vainly trying to put the flames out, and the local news van was filming a reporter a safe distance away.

This was how they were going to explain the kids' disappearance, she realized. A big tragic bus crash that people would forget in a decade or two. Probably if she looked in the town records, she'd find that some other terrible accident had befallen the kids picked for the big Devil's Night party thirty years before.

Left with no doubt whatsoever that this was a conspiracy, Millie crept onward, making sure that she wouldn't be seen as she passed the crash.

She finally made it back to her parents' house in the early grey dawn when the sun was just a rumor below the horizon. Exhaustion had dissolved her rage and terror into a disbelieving numbness. Her mother was sitting on the front steps, dozing against a porch pillar, one of the jack-o-lanterns she'd helped Millie carve sitting in her lap. Its candle had gone out. A wine glass and an empty bottle of merlot lay on the white-washed wooden planks beside her.

Millie shrugged off the blanket she'd pilfered from a beach house clothesline and shook her mother's shoulder. "Mom."

Mrs. Gibbs woke with a start, looked around, and then pressed a finger to her lips. Her eyes were very red, as if she'd been crying a long time that night.

"We have to be quiet. If anyone knows you're alive, they'll come after you again. I won't be able to do anything. I'm so sorry about all of this, honey."

"What the hell is going on?" Millie whispered, then flinched, expecting her mother to scold her for using a swear word.

But her mother didn't even seem to notice. "There's a cult here, and it's real, and Steve was a part of it long before I met him. And now we're all sucked in. I'm so sorry."

Millie felt her anger rise again. "Why didn't you tell me?"

Fresh tears welled in her mother's eyes. "I couldn't, honey. If you had known, you would have been so scared, and they'd have known that I told you. We'd both be dead now, and there would be nobody to protect your little brother and sister. I did the best I could think to do."

Millie wanted to scream at her, so she took care to speak as clearly and quietly as she could. "If you knew, why didn't you just take us and leave while he was away at work?"

Her mother's gaze turned distant, and when she spoke, her voice was hollow. "There was a ritual. I thought Steve and I were just going to lunch…but we weren't. They forced me. I'm bound here. I will literally die if I try to leave here with you or the twins. Steve had to promise a child to Dagon so he could rise in the ranks of the Order. He promised you. And you're still promised."

God. This was even more awful than she had imagined. "What happens now?"

"You have to leave here, tonight, and never come back. If they think you drowned in the ocean, the Order considers the promise fulfilled even though Dagon didn't get a child from our family. But if they find out you're alive, they'll try to get you. And if they can't get you, they'll demand that Steve give them a different child. And then he'll hand over your little brother or little sister."

Millie felt a shock run from her skull to the soles of her aching feet. "He wouldn't. He loves them."

Her mother gave a short, quiet, bitter laugh. She looked terrified. "He would. He'd hand over all of us if they asked him to. And he'd get married and start a new family with another woman he does his Prince Charming act for. He's not at all the man I thought he was. He's not even the man *you* think he is, and I know you never liked him much."

"He's a *monster*," Millie whispered.

Another quiet, bitter laugh. "This whole town is a monster factory, and it has been for a long, long time. But if you leave before they know you're alive, you and I and the twins stay safe. You can't call or write after you go; they read our mail, and they've tapped our phone. I wish it didn't have to be this way, but it does."

Millie felt completely lost. "Where do I go?"

"You're going to live with my cousin Penny in Fensmere, Mississippi. She knows a lot about monsters and cults and she can keep you safe."

"Cousin Penny?" Millie blinked. "You never mentioned her before, and now I'm supposed to go live with her?"

"It's not ideal. She's sort of a hermit. Not many people in the family really know her. I think she works as a private investigator? She tried to warn me about Steve, but I thought she was a lunatic." Her mother looked sad and deeply embarrassed. "I should have listened; everything she told me turned out to be true. She also told me that if any of my children were in danger, she would help. I called her from a payphone in Surfton the other night, and she said she'd send someone up here to collect you if you lived. And you did."

Her mother reached into her pocket for a lighter, re-ignited the candle in the jack-o-lantern. She stood and carefully set the pumpkin up on the broad porch railing beside their other jack-o-lantern and lit it, too.

At that, a car that Millie hadn't even noticed that was parked on the street a few houses down turned on its lights, flashed them three times, and turned them off again.

"And there's your ride." Her mother knelt to reach for something under the porch swing. When she stood up, she was holding Millie's old backpack—one she thought her mother had donated to Goodwill—and her violin case. "I packed essentials. Things Steve won't notice being gone. And a little money. I'll try to mail things from another town later."

The gravity of the situation finally hit Millie full-force. She was going to leave, maybe forever, and she might never see her mother again. She started to tear up. "I have to go now?"

"Yes. I'm sorry." Her mother set the luggage down and gave her a long hug. "Be good. A day won't pass where I don't think of you. I love you so much."

Tears flowed down Millie's cheeks in hot rivulets. "I love you, too."

"Go." Her mother helped her put on her backpack and gave her a gentle push.

Millie hurried across the lawns to the sedan. Someone inside flung the rear driver's side door open.

A black girl in pigtails who looked a little younger than Millie beckoned her excitedly. "Get in!"

Millie handed her the violin case. The girl grabbed it and scooted over on the seat so Millie could get in and shut the door behind her.

"Oh, cool, I play violin, too!" The girl exclaimed. "We could do duets later! Can you fiddle? I'm taking fiddle lessons from Miz Greene next year when she gets back—"

"Lena." The driver, a thirty-something woman with a short Afro haircut and hoop earrings, turned and gave the pigtailed girl a look. "What did I tell you?"

"Wash my hands?"

The woman rolled her eyes. "Context."

Lena brightened. "Oh. Right. Introduce myself first?"

"Yes."

The grinning girl turned back to Millie and stuck out her hand. "Hi, I'm Lena, and this is my mom Bess. Cousin Penny sent us to get you away from this terrible place. Cultists *suck*."

Millie shook her offered hand, feeling a bit like she'd fallen down a rabbit hole and this cheerful child was standing in for the Mad Hatter. "Hi. Good to meet you."

"Perfect!" Lena's mother started the car and pulled away from the curb. "As she says, I'm Bess. I'm Penny's investigative partner. She sends her regrets that she couldn't come get you herself, but she's got a distance vision problem that limits her driving. You'll meet her probably day after tomorrow. It's a really long drive to Fensmere, so I was thinking we could stop outside Harrisburg and get a hotel room. Your mom told Penny you love Halloween, and there are some good neighborhoods in the suburbs where I can take the two of you trick-or-treating. You up for that, Millie?"

Lena started excitedly whispering, "Say yes, say yes, say yes!"

"Sweet pea, don't pester her," Bess said. "She's been through a whole lot tonight. She might rather sleep, and we're not going to leave her by herself."

"I'd like that," Millie said. "But my pirate costume is all gross, and I lost my wig and my sword besides."

"It's okay! I brought a whole suitcase full of costumes, just in case!" Lena replied.

"But on that note," Bess said, "once we're out of cult territory, I'll find a truck stop where you can get a shower and change into fresh clothes if you like. Folks gonna think we tried to drown you if I drive around with you like this."

"I'd *definitely* like that," Millie said.

"Consider it done," said Bess.

Millie looked out the window just in time to see the "Welcome to Marsh Landing!" sign flash past and felt a wash of relief and sadness at the realization that she might never see it ever again.

Lena nudged her. "Hey. You know what today is? Besides it being Wednesday and Halloween, I mean."

Millie shook her head.

"It's the first day of the rest of your life!" Lena grinned excitedly.

Millie couldn't help but smile back. "Yeah, it sure is."

Visions of the Dream Witch

Quietly cursing our luck, I helped my cousin Jake limp down the muddy, rutted road. I wished we were back in New Orleans getting ready for the neighborhood Halloween party instead of slogging through the ass end of swamp country. But Jake and I got a little too curious about late-night shenanigans in a boarded-up warehouse near his father Rudy's auction house. We'd handled occult items during our three summers working there, so we both knew esoteric magic was real. But we never believed in the Outer Gods until we watched those damn fool cult members summon the Dream Witch Yidhra and her pack of enslaved shoggoths.

Beauty and her beasts. We did what we could with crowbars and gasoline. Yidhra vanished as the warehouse burned. She's truly something to behold, but you don't want to look her in the eye unless you want her inside your head. And you don't want to be bitten by a shoggoth unless you want to slowly, painfully turn into one.

By the time we set foot on that soggy back road, it had been 36 hours since one of the monsters munched on Jake's shoulder. The ER docs stitched him up and gave him an antibiotics shot. But his arm swelled and started breaking out in ugly dark boils that stank of brimstone. I called Beau LeRoux, a local professor who often bid on esoteric items we auctioned, hoping he might know what to do. LeRoux said only one person in the whole state might be able to help: Madame Caplette.

My cousin's whole arm puffed up like an andouille and turned black with those horrible boils. The bones in his hand were soft, rubbery. Worse, the swelling spread from his shoulder to his neck. He'd lost his voice and had a tough time breathing. The corruption was moving down his spine, and he could barely walk. I could tell it all hurt like absolute hell.

"She's gonna be able to help you, I know it," I told him.

He grunted and gave me a half-hearted thumbs-up.

Jake was the closest thing I had to a brother. We were nearly the same age. His parents took me to raise after my mom OD'd when I was just six. Adulterated heroin, back before it was cool. Dad was already serving a life sentence for dealing coke. Uncle Rudy's too softhearted to tell many hard truths to a little kid, but he never made any bones about what took my parents from me. Hate's a strong word, but that's how I feel about the turds who peddle poison. Jake loved my mom, too, and so we'd both been vigilant about watching for dealers in the neighborhood. We were certain that the cultists were selling meth, but we kinda lost our focus on that after Yidhra showed up.

I was glad he took after his mama and was a thin, wiry kid; if he'd been a linebacker type like Uncle Rudy, I couldn't have gotten him down the road. But woe betide any cocky dude who thought skinny meant weak; Jake boxed until he learned about chronic traumatic encephalopathy, and he had a left hook like a lightning bolt. I prayed he'd be able to keep his arm.

The road wound through a copse of oaks furred with Spanish moss and lichens to a sprawling blue ranch house with a red barn out back. A huge magnolia tree bloomed in the front yard, the white blossoms humming with bees. A stylized African statue of a man decorated entirely with cowry shells stood beside the galvanized steel mailbox. He held out a small bronze bowl that contained an assortment of blue glass beads; whether they were offers from or to visitors I couldn't tell, so I left them alone.

A knock-kneed girl of 9 or 10 in a purple jumper and bright pink Chuck Taylors came running around the side of the house, then slid to a dead stop when she saw us.

"Gran-maaaAAAA!" she hollered, pelting into the house, curly black pigtails bouncing. "There's people heeeere!"

A moment later, a stooped old woman came out of the house, squinting at us from behind thick old-fashioned bifocals. She leaned heavily on a staff of gnarled black wood. A cowry bracelet hung from her bony wrist.

"Who are you kids, and what do you want?" Her voice conveyed strength despite her physical frailty.

"I'm Pepper Mouton, and this is Jake Garza," I called back. "Beau LeRoux said he'd call about us?"

She stepped forward, looking over the tops of her spectacles at Jake's arm. "Lord have mercy. Get that boy into the house."

Once we got Jake settled on her couch, the old witch pulled a footstool over and began to examine my cousin's boils.

"Shoggoth?" she asked.

I nodded. "He got bit almost two days ago."

She rubbed her chin thoughtfully. "I can heal him, I reckon. But I'm a mite short of heart-juice for the potion. It's one more night to the new moon…it has to be taken when there's nothing but starlight. Monique can take you there, but you have to do the harvest. I'm too old to go running around in the bayou after that critter."

"What critter?" I asked.

"Sap Daddy. The beast come here with the Spaniards four hunnert years ago; they let it go in the swamp when it got too big to keep as a pet. And there it stayed, eating gators and getting bigger and bigger. When it died, something in the swamp kept it going. It's more plant than animal now, but that don't make it no less dangerous. Sap from its heart and some other bits and bobs are just the thing we need here."

"Can you keep Jake from getting any worse until we go out hunting?"

She nodded. "I 'spect I can."

Madame Caplette took me to a back workroom that had been outfitted in mismatched kitchen counters and cabinets with open shelving above. The old woman stood upon her tiptoes and took down a cardboard box.

"This here is what you'll need for the collectin'." She pulled out a copper-clad glass jug with a black rubber stopper and a galvanized steel funnel. Both looked like they had come from some backwoods moonshine still.

"And this is for the cuttin'." She unrolled a burlap bundle as long as my shinbone to reveal an African ceremonial knife. It had an elongated, leaf-shaped iron blade with a dark hardwood hilt and matching scabbard. The weapon looked positively ancient, and I could feel a strange vibration from it.

"Should I fill the whole jug?" I asked.

She nodded and pulled an old blue nylon gym bag from another shelf. "As close to full as you can get, but don't take more'n that, and don't waste none. Sap Daddy is a genuine gold-egg goose for us, and we need him healthy. Well, healthy as a thing like him can possibly be, I 'spose."

"Yes ma'am."

"Settle him down and cut one of the littlest heart-vines." She loaded everything into the bag. "He don't always come along easy. Monique is good with witch-song but she's real young. If the beast gets rambunctious, mind she don't get hurt. And don't you go dropping this knife over the side of the boat, or I'll make you go diving to find it again, you hear?"

"Yes ma'am. How do we find him?"

"Monique's real good at that. Use the old pole boat I got in the shed out back—motor noise scares him off."

The next night I dragged the old flat-bottomed skiff to the shallow water just after 11 p.m. There was no breeze to speak of. A piney haze in the air dimmed the stars. Without any moonlight, the stream bank seemed oppressively dark.

"So, once we find this thing, how do we catch it?" I asked Monique as we carefully stepped into the boat with our gear.

"I sing to him, and he gets still," she replied, setting her waterproof, hand-crank LED lantern on the wooden seat beside her.

"For real?" I put the old blue gym bag down in the cargo area, checked my shotgun and stowed it along the inner hull. Madame Caplette had warned me about big gators.

"For real." She dipped her paddle in the water.

I pushed off the bank with the long white fiberglass pole. "Bollywood tunes, or lullabies, or what?"

The girl rolled her eyes. "It likes old Spanish Christmas songs like '*Venid pastores*'. I guess they used to sing that to him back in the old days."

"So, no Lady Gaga?"

Monique gave me a sidelong squint that would've made Clint Eastwood proud. "Uh, *no*."

"That's good. 'Bad Romance' isn't really in my range."

"You're weird," she said.

"You have *no* idea," I replied.

The girl fell silent, and I kept pushing us along. The only sound was the faint swish of the water and the frogs calling to each other in the cattails. A few fireflies flitted to and fro, blinking come-hithers.

A woman laughed right behind me. I nearly dropped the pole in surprise. The boat rocked as I whirled around. The frogs went silent, startled by the sudden slap and splash of the hull. Nobody was there.

"What's the matter?" Monique frowned at me.

"Did you hear that?" I held my breath, trying to listen, scanning the weeds and dark water. Still nothing.

"Hear what?" she asked.

"That laugh."

"Uh, no...." The girl was staring at me as if she wasn't sure if I was messing with her or not.

"Seriously, you didn't hear that?"

"No, ma'am."

I swore under my breath and pushed the boat off again. "Never mind. Just my nerves, I guess."

Problem was, I didn't think I'd been all that nervous. Not enough to start hearing things, anyway. Jake's life depended on this. Pressure? Sure. But this was something a 9-year-old could do. Had done several times, apparently. How bad could it be?

"Oh, there's plenty that could go bad tonight." Yidhra's voice. Directly behind me.

I cussed and turned again, holding the pole like a spear. My heart was thudding. "Where the hell are you?"

Her head broke the surface a few yards behind the boat, just beyond my pole's reach. She smiled. "I'm right here. Or am I?"

"What do you mean?" My voice shook.

"Maybe I'm not here at all." Yidhra smoothly breaststroked forward, graceful as a naiad, still keeping her distance. Her long black hair fanned out in the water behind her. "Maybe I'm just a hallucination. Maybe you caught a virus that's eating away at your brain, and you're going crazy."

"Uh, ma'am, who are you talking to?" Monique sounded worried.

I swallowed, my throat suddenly dry.

"Or maybe I'm here, and your songbird just can't see me," Yidhra continued. "And she won't see me even when I cut her skinny little throat."

"Leave her alone." I gripped the pole with my left hand and bent down to pick up my Mossberg with my right. I trained the shotgun on Yidhra, who just laughed at me.

"What's going on?" Monique sounded genuinely scared. "Is—is someone out there?"

I looked back at the girl. Her brown eyes were huge, and her cheeks were wet with frightened tears.

"Don't worry." I tried to sound calm and confident. "There's a problem, but it's *my* problem, all right? Just get us to Sap Daddy."

Monique nodded and wiped her face. "Okay."

"I might say some stuff to my friend in the water," I continued. "Just…just ignore it, ok?"

The request sounded stupid the moment I made it, but Monique simply nodded again, all her eye-rolling sassiness gone. One good thing about kids who've been raised around witchcraft is that while they might be annoyingly cavalier about some stuff, they know to take it seriously when real monsters come calling. Or at least they'll go with real monsters as plausible, and not immediately assume that the person in the boat with you has just transformed into a hallucinating, gun-waving lunatic.

"A lunatic without a moon to howl at." Yidhra laughed again. "How ironic. How sad."

I set my shotgun down and poled us away from her fast as I could, my shoulders straining with my effort, but the death goddess easily kept pace with the boat.

"Shove off," I said.

"You're just heartbroken over your cousin, aren't you?" Her voice was husky with fake sympathy. "Here you are, trying *so* hard to save him, and every minute that ticks off the clock is a minute he's closer to death. He's suffering so much, Pepper, so much more than you know. And you've put his future in the hands of a little girl and an old witch. Do you really think they can save him?"

"Do you have a point?" I spat.

"I think it would be a mercy to put him out of his misery," she replied. "And take his soul for safekeeping."

"Go to hell."

"Perhaps I should put the old woman down. Perhaps I'm at her house, right this very minute, and before you can get your little boat turned around I'll have her scattered all over her garden. You can watch Jake die horribly tomorrow."

My heart was pounding so hard that my vision was shaking. I stared at Yidhra, who was floating on her back, just her face and naked breasts clear of the water. "Why would you do that?"

She shrugged. "Because I can. Because you and your cousin disrupted my plans. I'm merely returning the favor."

"If you hurt Jake or Madame Caplette," I growled, "I won't rest until I've destroyed you. I will see you burn."

Yidhra laughed uproariously at that, splashing merrily. I focused on poling the boat as quickly as I could while Yidhra began to detail all the grotesque ways she would kill my loved ones, and *their* loved ones. I wished I had a pair of earplugs, but I knew she'd wormed her way into my brain. Not even a jet engine would drown out her voice.

We reached the mouth of the stream, which opened into the dark maze of a bald cypress swamp. The tree limbs dripped with Spanish moss. The water here was stagnant, the surface thick with duckweed and drifting mats of ragged algae. I could smell rotting vegetation and the rankness of reptile dung, either from gators or something much bigger.

"...in Tepes' time, a good impaler could hammer in a stake without destroying any major organs," Yidhra said, "and a young, healthy victim could suffer for two or even three days before he died. But I've heard that with modern piercing techniques and saline and antibiotics you can keep your playmate aware and in agony for nearly twice as long. I think I'll try that with your Uncle Rudy—he's not that young, but he seems pretty strong, don't you think?"

A terrible image rose in my mind, a psychic sucker punch: my uncle hanging screaming from a huge wooden spike that someone had rammed up under his ribcage and out through his shoulder. My senses spun with vertigo, and I fell to my knees in the boat. Fortunately, I didn't lose my pole. Or my dinner.

"What happened?" Monique looked even more scared than before.

"Just got dizzy." I blinked to try to clear my vision and got to my feet. "Where do we go from here?"

"That way." She pointed out into the darkness. "I can feel him."

I kept on poling the boat through the debris and cypresses as Yidhra's descriptions grew even more horrifying and vivid. Sometimes the water around us turned into a lake of blood and dismembered bodies. Vegetal rot turned to a charnel house stench. Sometimes the Spanish moss transformed into festoons of steaming entrails. The trees became a thousand crooked gallows decorated with the corpses of the condemned. Sometimes the entire landscape around me looked like a Hieronymus Bosch nightmare.

"I'm…having a hard time seeing straight," I finally told Monique. "Make sure I'm going the right way, okay? If it seems like I'm going to wreck the boat, say something. *Please.*"

The girl looked back at me, and I flinched. It looked like someone had scraped her face off with a length of razor wire.

"Are you okay?" The part of my head that was buying Yidhra's illusion marveled at how well Monique could speak without any lips.

I shook my head. "It's my problem, not yours. Just don't let me wreck us."

A little while later, she inhaled sharply.

"What is it?" I couldn't glimpse anything but the landscape of carnage.

"It's him. He's here, I know it."

"Where?" I strained to see past the bloody veil.

"I dunno, I can't—"

The girl shrieked and something big and strong rammed the bottom of our boat, knocking it sideways and suddenly I was plunging into the warm, sticky gore. I went under completely for a moment, fighting against what felt like a dozen dead hands grasping my arms and clothes, but I managed to surface, spitting foul gore from my mouth.

Monique was still screeching in panic. The girl definitely had a sturdy set of lungs.

"It'll be okay!" I hollered up at her, part of me wondering if I was telling her a terrible lie. I still couldn't see the beast, but I could feel the vibrations of something huge pulling itself across the muddy swamp bottom. "You know what to do…sing to it!"

I heard her take a deep breath, and I figured she'd just start screaming again—hell, if I'd been in her situation they could have strapped me to the roof of a fire truck and used me as a siren—but what came out was a beautiful soprano note, a little shaky at first, but it got stronger and stronger and became a sound of such transcendent clarity you could compare it to the purest stream in the mountains above Shangri-la or the gleam of Caladbolg's steel or the glitter of the Hope Diamond and all those other things would seem mundane and unimpressive. Monique had the kind of voice that could make the most cynical, hard-minded atheist instantly believe in a benevolent higher power, believe in *anything*.

She held the note a little longer, then took another breath and began to sing an old Spanish Christmas song. I didn't understand the lyrics, but the words didn't matter. The power was all in her voice, and as Monique's music flowed over me, Yidhra's horrible vision evaporated like fog in sunshine. The gore around me became innocuous swamp water, and what had seemed to be zombie hands grabbing at my legs was just a tangle of common riverweeds.

I looked up, and found myself staring up into a set of toothed jaws the size of Madame Caplette's Volkswagen. I'd have been petrified if the sight of the monster wasn't such a welcome relief from Yidhra's visions. It was the skeleton of a dragon reanimated by the swamp. Creaking green vines were muscle and sinew linking the ancient bones. Moss bearded the dragon's jaw and huge scarlet rose mallow flowers bloomed in caches of muddy debris on its back and sides. I could see between its ribs, and where the dragon's flesh heart should have been was a knot of dark, shiny vines that pulsed with a faint blue glow.

Monique was standing ramrod straight in the boat, giving the song everything she had. I caught her eye and she pointed at the gear bag with a *get on with it!* expression.

I splashed back to the boat for the bag, slung it across my back, and climbed the beast's slippery vines to reach the heart. The heart was blocked by some stray vegetation; I cut as little of it away as possible, just enough so I could squeeze the jug and funnel into the chest cavity. I positioned the funnel beneath one thin, pulsing black vine, then slit it with the tip of the knife.

Black sap began to ooze from the core of the vine down into the funnel and the jug. The fishy odor was much more pungent in this fresh dragon molasses. My eyes watered. The vine clogged after a little while and I had to make another cut. My thigh muscles began to ache from the effort of clinging to the rib, but I hung on until the jug was full. I carefully corked the jug, slipped it and the knife and funnel back in the gym bag, and slid down to the water.

Once I was back in the boat, Monique continued caroling as I poled us away back toward the stream, avoiding the mossy wrecks of other boats that had ventured into the swamp after Sap Daddy.

"Do you think you can keep singing long enough for us to get home?" I asked. Whatever witchcraft the girl was able to weave in her music, it was doing a fabulous job of keeping Yidhra out of my head. I knew Monique couldn't keep it up forever, but I'd enjoy what peace I could get while it lasted.

Monique nodded, looking a little mischievous. She took a deep breath, and started belting out "This is Halloween".

I smiled and began to sing along with her.

We were on "Monster Mash" when we arrived. Madame Caplette was waiting for us on the stream bank, looking impatient. "Why you singing that, girl? I told you not to waste your skills on them silly songs!"

Looking innocent, Monique pointed at me.

I just shrugged. "She's helping me out with a little problem tonight." I stepped out of the boat with the gear bag. "We got the sap; you want it?"

The old witch ignored the bag and frowned up at me. "'A little problem' my bony posterior! Bend down here so I can take a look at your eyes, girl."

I did as she asked, and she took off her spectacles and peered into my eye, holding up her kerosene lantern for a better look.

Monique hopped out of the boat and peered at my face. "Ooh, your eyes have gotten all purple! They look like grapes!"

"Well, now, when was you gonna tell me you're possessed?" Madame Caplette's sharp tone of disapproval made my innards clench.

"Well, now, since when do *you* care?" I shot back. "It's my problem, not yours."

"It gets to be my problem right quick if your head starts a' spinnin' while I'm in the middle of the ritual! If I get distracted, your cousin gets *dead*. Do you want that?"

I flinched, realizing I'd been an idiot. "No, ma'am. I'm sorry."

Her expression softened. "Got a notion of who's in you?"

"Yidhra." The name tasted like cigarette ash on my tongue.

"And the beast that bit your cousin, was it in thrall to her?"

"Yeah."

"And you didn't think to mention that?" She scowled. "You didn't think that all this would have been a thing I needed to know right when you brung him here?"

Heat rose in my cheeks. "No."

"Lord Almighty." She lowered her lantern and sighed at me, shaking her head. "Come on to the house. I got something that'll keep it from getting any worse. It ain't a permanent solution, but it'll work for now. Looks like I gotta rethink everything, because it ain't just Jake who needs healing."

She took me to a back bedroom where she unlocked a large mahogany jewelry chest and pulled out a necklace made of blue glass beads with a large round turquoise pendant. When she held the necklace out to me, I realized the beads and stone were carved to look like eyes.

"Wear it close to your heart," she said.

"Yes ma'am." I slipped the necklace on over my head and tucked it under my tee shirt. The moment the stone and glass touched my bare skin, I felt the same kind of cool washing-over relief that Monique's song had given me in the swamp.

I helped Madame Caplette set up a black iron cauldron on a tripod over a pine log fire in the middle of a big circle of packed earth in the back yard. We gathered fresh herbs from her garden, and put the dragon molasses, plants, a jug of rum, some silver nitrate powder, and a whole lot of black pepper into the cauldron to boil.

Next, she had me and Monique dig two post holes inside the arcane circle just beyond the worst of the heat from the fire and pound sturdy wooden 6x6s into both of them. The posts were standard pressure-treated lumber like you'd use for a deck, but someone had screwed D-rings into the sides. I'd seen the same kind of thing in someone's bondage dungeon once.

"You're not gonna tie us up out here, are you?" I joked nervously.

The old witch looked grave. "Matter of fact, I have to. The evil in you ain't gonna let go without a fight."

I held my breath and nervously twisted my wrists in their ropes as Madame Caplette started the ritual. The old witch raised an owl-feathered rattle made from a dried gourd lashed to a human radius bone and the ceremonial knife. She began to chant, stomp and dance around the potion bubbling in the cauldron. A bucket of dry ice for cooling the finished potion sent an eerie low fog across the ground beyond the fire. Her motions were practiced and utterly confident. She slashed the air with the knife as if she were cutting down every last one of the forces of evil.

Jake moaned and struggled against his post. I couldn't understand much of the chant, but I caught enough to know she was calling on the whole *guédé* loa family to help us fend off Yidhra and her minions. Loas don't always have good will towards humankind. But they are of the Earth, and Yidhra pretends to be but is not. This was a clear supernatural turf war if ever there was one. Madame Caplette brought all her authority to the chant, and she wielded an ancient, powerful magic that was downright scary. Hairs rose on my arms and the back of my neck, as if a thunderstorm were gathering above us, but the sky was clear.

A shock rocketed through me as if Jake had slammed me with one of his haymaking left hooks.

Suddenly there I was, back in the burning warehouse, facing Yidhra in all her terrible beauty.

"I've seen into your heart." She smiled at me. "I know exactly what you want, Pepper. It can all be yours if you give yourself to me."

She showed a vision of me holding court for socialites and politicians in a grand old house in Lakewood. Everybody knew my name because I'd personally funded all the drug rehab programs, homeless shelters, and job programs. All the misery and poverty in the city was gone because of me. I was smart, respected, cool. Any old thing I decided to wear became that season's fashion. Pop stars like Beyoncé wanted to meet me. People asked for my autograph at parties. Our city was no longer the punchline of jokes about drunks or hurricanes. New Orleans shone as the brightest diamond in America's crown, and I was its princess.

I saw it all so clearly, and I wanted it so badly. I just had to let Yidhra devour me, heart and soul, and the dream would come true. But deep down I knew it would be an illusion that only existed inside my own head. Because if the dark goddess could do all that, why hadn't it been done?

"No," I said.

"If you refuse me, your family will suffer like none before."

She showed me visions of Jake screaming, his skin dripping off his body as the shoggoth corruption took hold and crushed his bones to mush before he became a formless, blister-eyed monstrosity. I saw Rudy flayed, his arms and legs smashed with a sledgehammer. I saw his wife Lori chopped to pieces in our basement. I saw myself doing all these terrible things to my aunt and uncle. The goddess would take hold of me and force me to torture them if I refused her. I'd end up locked away in some asylum, mad and savage and hated until I finally died.

I grabbed Yidhra by her long, beautiful hair and dragged her with me into the heart of the warehouse fire. She screamed and clawed at my face as we both burned, our skin blistering and blackening. The agony of it took the air from my lungs, but I had to protect my family. I *had* to. The pain of immolation was worse than anything I'd ever imagined, but I held the shrieking goddess in the flames. My will was stronger than flesh and bone.

I came back to the real world, gagging as Madame Caplette poured the hot, bitter, tarry potion down my throat.

"You got to swallow it!" she ordered.

I did as she told me. My clothes were soaked through with sweat, and my wrists and arms ached, raw from my fighting against the ropes all night. The eye-stone necklace still hung solid and cool around my neck. Dawn was breaking through the trees, and the early morning sky was lit in delicate reds and purples.

My cousin sat slumped over, still bound to his post. But he was breathing. I wasn't sure but it seemed like the swelling in his arm had gone down.

"Jake," I called. "You still with us?"

He slowly raised his head. "That was a real messed-up dream I just had." His voice was hoarse, but strong.

"I think y'all are both on the mend," said Madame Caplette.

"You know she's gonna come back, right?" Jake stared at me, his eyes clear and unafraid. "She got a taste of both our souls, and she ain't gonna give up so easy."

"Well, she can't be more persistent than any of the effin' narco gangs who keep coming into our neighborhood, can she?" I replied. "If she wants another ass-kicking, by gods we'll give her one."

Jake smiled. "That we will, cuz. That we will."

What Dwells Within

"We should *not* be out right now." My ferret familiar Pal's telepathic voice was strained with anxiety. He peered out our borrowed Toyota's passenger window, whiskers twitching. Scanning the late afternoon clouds for signs of the Virtus Regnum, no doubt.

I couldn't blame him. If my protective spell failed, the Regnum's huge enforcer spirits would tear the autumn Ohio sky open and burn us to ashes. And they wouldn't care too much about who else got expunged in the process. Humans were little more than vermin to them at the best of times. Whatever greater power in the universe had put them in charge of protecting the Earth from all the eldritch horrors out there must have done it to punish their species. On the bright side, their distaste for humanity made them totally unimpressed with any bribes that even powerful wizards could think up. So most of the time you could count on them to treat everyone the same: with near-complete contempt. But at least we were all equal in their law-abiding eyes.

Except me, Jessie Shimmer. I'd slain one of their kind. Entirely in self-defense, mind you, but that detail didn't matter to them. I'd done something no human was supposed to be able to do, and so I was a threat to be dealt with. Public enemy number one. Dead woman walking.

"It'll be fine," I said aloud as I turned south on High Street, passing Graeter's Ice Cream and a couple of upscale wine and candle shops in trendy brick storefronts, all decorated in strings of toothy orange paper jack-o-lanterns for Halloween.

I could have answered him telepathically. But that required a bit more concentration, so I saved it for when we were around other people. A seemingly one-sided conversation with a ferret tends to make folks think you've had a psychotic break, and then everything gets awkward.

Vague premonition itched like hives in the back of my mind, worse now than it had when I woke from a nightmare at 5 a.m. I couldn't remember the alarming dream, not even one detail, so I'd tried to ignore the whole thing. But the psychic irritation just kept building until I wanted to slam my head through a wall. *Something* was up, but neither meditation nor the couple of divination spells I'd tried gave me any clarity. My boyfriend Cooper was off with his little brothers and I didn't want to interrupt family time with something I figured I could handle fine by myself. Eventually.

Sometimes having Talent sucks. Magic is seldom straightforward when you need it to be. So I gave Mother Karen—thank God she'd been willing to give us a place to stay—a bullshit story about wanting to take a jog around Antrim Park and borrowed her Corolla to see if being out and about on a mild Sunday evening would give me any relief or get me any answers. Karen's a sharp witch and normally she'd twig to my lie right quick, but a couple of her foster kids were having a fight over the TV and she was so preoccupied with them that she just handed me the keys.

I'd put my shotgun in the trunk, just in case, but it wouldn't do any good if the Regnum paid us a visit.

"We should be staying put until the meeting with the Governing Circle," Pal fussed.

"I know." He wasn't wrong; if Circle leader Riviera Jordan were willing to offer us safe haven, we'd be relatively okay staying in the city. Relatively. Riviera seemed like a fair lady and she knew I'd gotten a raw deal. But she hadn't made her decision yet, and going against the Regnum was an awfully big one. If I landed us in some kind of mess before the meeting and pissed off anyone else in the Circle, she would almost certainly wash her hands and tell us to get the hell out of Columbus.

"This is really quite dangerous," Pal said. "And if you wanted to go to the park, we should have gone north."

"I know. We're not going to the park." The buzz of premonition had moved from the back of my head into my chrysoberyl eye, and the scars around it were starting to itch a little. A flashback memory of fiery demon's blood spraying across the left side of my face made me wince. My enchanted stone ocularis was damned handy for seeing all manner of things that normal humans couldn't spy, but getting my eye melted out of my head was a memory I wished I could purge.

My left hand and forearm were getting a pins-and-needles feeling, too. The same demon had bitten that arm off just below the elbow, and one thing led to another and that arm became a torch of hellfire for a while. No more fire—thank God; constantly setting off smoke detectors is *not* a good way to keep a low profile—but now I had an eerie white replica of my lower arm that I couldn't definitely say was flesh. I'd undergone an hours-long healing and exorcism ritual in Switzerland, and the ceremony was supposed to re-grow my arm and restore it to normal, but the magic just couldn't quite get there. Too much demonic residue in my system.

Eerie or not, I wasn't about to complain about getting a working limb back. Sure, it was cold as a refrigerated corpse and glowed faintly blue in the dark, but I could feel through it just fine. I kept telling myself that functionality was what mattered. Most days I told myself I still wore my magically flame-proofed gray opera glove just in case it flared up again, but frankly seeing that creepy white thing at the end of my arm made my skin crawl.

Besides, if I touched anyone with the glove off and I wasn't paying attention, there was a chance I might drag the both of us into my personal hell dimension. Awkward. Very awkward.

"Where *are* we going, then?" Pal asked.

"Trust me, I'll let you know as soon as I figure that one out."

He made an exasperated squeak and curled up on the grey passenger seat in a tight, frustrated ball, his nose buried under his fluffy sable tail. He looked completely adorable, but now was not the time to tell him that. Probably he was wishing he were in his grizzly bear form so he could wrestle me for the wheel and get us turned around. But then he'd be far too big to fit in the compact car, and besides, he needed a strong electrical jolt to trigger his shape-shift. We kept a stun gun around for that and it wasn't pleasant. I'd recently worked out an electroshock spell, but that wasn't any nicer than the zapper.

I'd have hated to be in his position. He was my first and only familiar, and when I got him I didn't realize that intelligent familiars are all indentured souls trapped in animal bodies. It's kind of a horrifying system if you learn much about it, but familiars are so handy that nobody wants to know that part. Pal would have gotten freed eventually once he'd served a fairly long sentence for a mistake he'd made when he was young, but I'd screwed that up by getting on the Regnum's shitlist. We were both outlaws now. Sticking by me meant his life was always going to be in danger. And in many ways he *had* to stick by me. We were still magically linked as master and familiar and nobody but I could hear his telepathic speech. The magic binding familiars is powerful, and I didn't know how to fix things so he'd be entirely free. And I couldn't ever pay him back for everything he'd already done for me. If I thought about it too hard I had Beck's "Loser" playing as the soundtrack inside my head, and that wouldn't do either of us any good, so I just tried to not think about it.

"I'm not crazy," I told him. "Well, okay, I *am* sort of having the crazies today, but this is me trying to fix that. I'm having a premonition I can't figure out, and I'm hoping something jumps out at me."

"Why didn't you just say so?" He sounded cross.

"Because I figured it would sound dumb when I said it out loud."

"When has that ever stopped you before?"

"Oh, bite me," I said affectionately. If he was snarking at me, that meant he couldn't be *too* angry.

I followed my itchy instincts and turned left onto North Broadway. Soon we were approaching the bridge over I-71.

Wait. There was something on the overpass fence. But I only caught a glimpse of it through my ocularis; my flesh eye hadn't seen a thing. I clicked on my hazards and pulled over to the side of the road, annoying the driver of a little yellow Volkswagen Beetle behind me. He honked indignantly and zoomed around me. Nobody else was coming from either direction.

I stared at the spot; through my ocularis it was an indistinct blur slowly moving up the fence. Man-sized, maybe? I started blinking through other enchanted views through the stone. Blur…blur…darker blur…bright blur… and suddenly I saw a thin, shirtless white guy with brown dreadlocks and blue basketball shorts struggling to climb the chain link fence, his flip-flops giving him little purchase on the galvanized wire.

"Holy shit, that's Kai," I told Pal.

"Where?" my familiar peered around, confused.

"On the fence. Someone turned him invisible. *Mostly* invisible. Come on."

Pal hopped onto my shoulder as I killed the engine. I hadn't seen Kai in months; I'd sublet a room in his run-down Victorian rental for a few days while I was recuperating after the demon fight. I was seriously messed up in pretty much every way you can imagine, but he had a little crush on me anyhow, and he'd really been a huge help when I'd sorely needed it. Bit of a stoner, but a good guy. A little naïve, but he was still a teenager after all. As far as I knew, he didn't hang out with anyone else who knew magic; who could have turned him invisible?

"Hey, Kai!" I stepped out of the car, pocketed the keys, and shut the door. "What are you doing out here?"

"He said…he said…" Kai muttered. His voice was slurred like he was drunk. Or under a magical compulsion.

I waited for a silver Honda Odyssey minivan to pass and then jogged across the street. Kai still seemed determined to get up the fence. "What did he say?"

"He said jump off a bridge…he said jump off a bridge…"

"Whoa, no!" I reached up and grabbed his hairy leg. "Come on down from there. Let's go get some coffee."

"Well, I can see him now," Pal remarked inside my mind. "The spell fails at close range. Whoever cast that didn't do much of a job."

Fast and sloppy, I thought back. *But it only had to work well enough to keep anyone from seeing him until he'd thrown himself over into traffic.*

It would be a quick death, maybe, but I cringed to imagine the massive freeway pile-up that would follow. What if he splattered across the windshield of a car full of little kids? Jesus. Even if they survived the wreck, they'd never get over seeing something like that. Whoever did this definitely wanted Kai gone, but they were both too lazy to do it themselves *and* perverse enough to want his death to cause mayhem. That was a kind of twisted you didn't see every day. I liked Kai and owed him a solid. But even if I'd hated his guts, I wanted to get to the bottom of all this, because whoever would cast a spell like this deserved to get their ass kicked. A *lot*.

"He said jump off a bridge," Kai insisted, clinging to the fence with white knuckles, trying to pull his leg from my grasp.

I had to do something to break the enchantment and free him. But I didn't have any spell ingredients on me. What could I use? I scanned the ground and spied a brown sparrow's feather sticking out of a wind-drifted pile of dead grass and dust in the gutter.

"Bingo." I released his leg, plucked the feather, and stepped back to concentrate on the chant.

Ubiquemancy is the art of finding and using magic in everyday objects. It's just a *little* tricky. And I hate performing it out in the open where random people can see. It isn't just that public displays of magic are of those universally *verboten* things. It's that ubiquemancy looks hella goofy. It's the magical equivalent of speaking in tongues, and once I start a chant for all I know I could end up barking like a dog or clucking like a chicken. I don't have an overabundance of dignity, but some things you just feel better about doing in private.

I took a deep breath and let it out slowly, trying to center myself.

"Don't you dare start laughing at me if this falls flat," I muttered to Pal.

"Perish the thought." He was gazing at Kai struggling up the wire. At least the kid wasn't making fast progress, so we had a bit of time. "Serious situation is serious."

I closed my eyes, focused on the feather in my cupped hands, took another deep breath, and started speaking words for freedom and release. The magic kicked in smoothly and ancient, lost words started spilling from my lips. I could feel the little feather heating on my palm, smell it starting to burn. My chant grew louder, stronger, and I could feel the magic it carried pushing against the spell binding Kai. Tension rose, higher and higher, as the invisible forces torqued against each other.

Suddenly the feather exploded with a *Pop!* and Kai gave a startled yelp.

"Whoa, what the hell!" His eyes were huge and panicked. It looked like I'd managed to nix both the compulsion and the lazy invisibility.

"Where am I?" he asked.

"You're on the North Broadway overpass," I told him, trying to sound soothing. "Just come down from there, but go easy. Your body might not do what you want it to for a little while."

I helped him down off the fence, and he stood there gasping on shaky legs, looking gray-faced and frail. Like a confused old man. For the first time, I noticed that his right eye was purpled and swollen like he'd taken a solid punch in the face sometime in the past few hours.

"What happened?" I asked him. "Who did this to you?"

"I...I don't..." He shook his head, but then his eyes seemed to focus, and I could practically see the memories swarming back into his mind. "Oh, shit. Oh shit shit *shit*."

"Dude, stop panicking!" I put a comforting hand on his shoulder. "Deep breaths. Tell me what happened."

"They took Alice! Oh Jesus, we gotta find her, Jessie, they're gonna do something terrible to her!"

"Slow down, bro. Who's Alice? Who took her?"

"She...I met her a few weeks ago. She's like you; she knows magic. I figured from the start she knew some dangerous dudes, but...well, we got this jeweled statue of Santa Muerte that we were trying to sell off. I mean, the thing creeped me out and I wanted to just leave it in an alley someplace but she was all 'We can get good coin for this,' so—"

"Wait." There were some perfectly nice people in the world who prayed to lovely Saint Death, but most of the ones I'd met personally were either necromancers or hired guns working for the narco cartels. And nice wasn't part of their job descriptions. "What were you doing with a statue of Santa Muerte?"

"Uh." He scratched his scalp nervously. "After you left, I rented your room to this guy named Halulu, and he came up with the idea to do a deal with some gang bangers to make some cash for the rent. I thought it was just going to be weed but it was meth and the whole thing went sideways."

"Oh, Mensa is bereft of this lad, and its members weep," Pal intoned from my shoulder.

"A drug deal?" I said. "For God's sake. Really?"

"Yeah, okay, I know, okay?" Kai looked embarrassed. "Halulu had this way of making it seem totally reasonable, but I know it wasn't. I'm not *stupid*."

He rubbed his arms as if he were remembering something terrifying. "Some really freaky shit went down. One of the gang dudes got shot; I spoke to his ghost and there was this *thing* in the room with us...."

He trailed off, looking horrified, but shook himself and continued. "Alice sort of took charge afterward and helped us get out of the mess. We were able to pay back the guys in Detroit and it was all good. I mean, except for the dead guy. But all we had left over from the deal was the statue, and we still needed to pay the rent. So Alice started checking around, friends of friends, you know? And someone was interested in the statue. And they came to the house this afternoon and…oh God."

He went pale, his lips a clamped line.

"Could they have been friends of the dead guy?" I prompted.

Kai shook his head, his dreadlocks brushing his shoulders. "He was a murderer—his ghost told me so—but he was regular, you know? Maybe a sociopath or whatever but he was just a guy. But the ones who showed up…I don't think they were even human. They were just trying to look like people. They wanted the statue but they also wanted Alice, and when I tried to stop them the boss guy backhanded me across the room like I was nothing and told me to jump off a bridge. And…I don't know much after that."

I paused. Kai didn't know *any* Talents before me. He hadn't been mixed up in anything more dangerous or illegal than a pair of sad marijuana plants he and his roommates were growing in the basement. Could my brief stay at his house have made him vulnerable to darker forces and set all this in motion? I didn't voice my concern to Pal; he'd tell me that I couldn't think that way or else I'd drive myself crazy and blah blah blah. But I *was* thinking that way, and consequently I felt even worse for Kai. Even if he *had* been a dumbass.

"I guess Alice means a whole lot to you?"

"Hell yeah." He had a dreamy look in his brown eyes that made me certain he was hard in love with her. "She's great; you'd like her, Jessie."

"I'm sure." If she was as much of a loose cannon as I suspected she was, we'd either get on like a house on fire or want to stab each other in the face. "Let's go back to your place, and we can start tracking her down."

Kai's rental on East Avenue was a huge old Victorian single in desperate need of a fresh paint job; the glow of the setting sun didn't make it look any better. The broad front porch had surely been stately a hundred years before. Now the floorboards were warped and the railings were as broken and gray as a meth addict's teeth. Ragged lawn chairs surrounded a squat red plastic table covered in crumpled Pabst Blue Ribbon cans. Cigarette butts spilled from an old brown glass ashtray. A pair of pumpkins guarded either side of the front door; someone had crudely scrawled triangular eyes and jack-o-lantern mouths on each one with a black Sharpie marker. An unopened carving kit lay on the boards beside the leftmost pumpkin.

"Ah, hovel sweet hovel." Pal's telepathic voice dripped with sarcasm.

"Your roommates around?" I asked Kai.

"Nah, Mikey and Patrick went down to Athens for a Halloween party. They'll probably roll in tomorrow morning."

"Just as well," I replied. "They probably couldn't have stopped the guys who took Alice, either."

"Assuming that they'd even *try*," Pal grumped to me. "Neither of those two seemed to have an overabundance of bravery."

Shush, I thought back.

"Ah, shit, the door's open." Kai ran up onto the porch and pushed into the house. "Dammit!"

"What?" I called.

"Someone stole our shit!" He pulled at his dreadlocks, looking like he was going to cry. "The flatscreen and our game stuff are gone! Today is just fuckin' *fired*."

No surprise that someone had seized the opportunity to loot the house. You could leave your door unlocked in some neighborhoods, but North Campus was not one of them. "Deep breaths. I can help you with that, too, but let's worry about Alice first, okay?"

"Yeah." He rubbed his eyes with the heels of his hands. "It's just stuff, right? I should be glad to be alive right now."

"But speaking of stuff, do you have any of Alice's I could use to try to track her?" I asked. "Like a brush with her hair, or some piece of clothing she's worn?"

"Sure, yeah. Come on in."

I followed him into the living room. His battered thrift store entertainment center was empty and toppled by the thieves' haste to leave, as were the makeshift bricks-and-boards shelves that had held his movie and game collection. The rest of the room looked okay, or at least okay by college bro standards. In some guys' places you'd be hard-pressed to know if they had been ransacked or not.

But a red gleam on the floor by the bricked-up fireplace caught my attention. I stepped closer, and saw a glittering ruby surrounded by dark faceted onyx on a shattered fragment of bronze. It was maybe as big as the lid of an Altoids tin and looked to be part of Santa Muerte's dress. And it was lying in a puddle of dark ooze.

"Did anyone throw or drop the statue over here?" I asked Kai.

He shook his head. "Sorry, I don't remember."

I grabbed a ballpoint pen from off the cluttered coffee table and used it to flip the fragment over. The edges of the metal looked pale and twisted, as though something had wrenched the bronze apart. On the floor where it had lain, I saw a shred of grayish, leathery membrane, and I caught a strong whiff of amniotic brine and brimstone from the ooze.

"Well, this is unexpected," Pal whispered.

"There was an egg inside the statue," I said to Kai. "And whatever hatched was strong enough to tear the metal apart."

"Whoa," he replied. "So *that's* what was making that scratching noise we were hearing. We thought we had a mouse someplace."

What could have been hiding in there? I thought to Pal. *My knowledge of Mexican magical lore is pretty rusty, but I don't remember anything about Santa Muerte's figures containing any icky little piñata surprises like this.*

"My guess is it's some kind of devil larvae that survives through spiritual parasitism," he said inside my mind. "It can slowly grow inside the statue, feeding off the prayer energy directed towards it by worshippers."

That's pretty sneaky, I thought back. *Even for a devil.*

"The question I'm most concerned with is: where did it go after it hatched?" Pal said.

"Yeah. We don't want whatever was in that statue running around loose," I replied. "Maybe the guys who grabbed Alice took the hatchling with them, but maybe they didn't. Let me try using some of the fragments to track it…."

Kai lent me a pair of pliers to pick up the gooey bit of membrane. I'm not squeamish, but you just don't want to touch fluids from any diabolic creature unless you know for sure what it can do. I'd been possessed before and it's not fun.

I closed my eyes, focused on the membrane, and started chanting old words for "find". I'd done tracking spells before to find devils; generally all my trouble came after I found them. As the words spilled from my lips, I started to get a hazy image of a two-story house—

—*Wham!*

The blocking magic felt like an armored fist smashing into my forehead, and for a moment, my vision went entirely white. I came awake sprawled on my back on the dirty wooden floor. Pal had leaped off my shoulder when I fell and was safe on the nearby ottoman.

"What happened?" my familiar asked.

"Junior's protected," I croaked, hoping the room would stop spinning sometime soon. "We gotta try for Alice."

Kai peered down at me, looking worried. "Can I get you anything?"

"A Coke or Pepsi would be great," I replied. "And some of Alice's hair if you have it. *Head* hair, please, and thank you."

Kai jogged into the kitchen and brought back a cold can of Faygo cola. "It's all we got, sorry."

"Thanks." I sat up and took the drink, hoping he wasn't secretly a Juggalo. Drug dealing and dark magic I could handle, but terrible taste in music might make me question our friendship.

"Are you okay?" Pal asked me as Kai went upstairs to look for Alice's hairbrush. "You're quite pale and rather sweaty."

"I'm fine. Just feeling kinda shaky from the spell block. Sugar and caffeine should fix me up, though." I took a long swig from the can, then let out the inevitable belch.

Kai soon returned with a foofy ball of ash-blonde hair. "Will this work?"

"It should." I cupped the blonde wad in my hands and began the chant. Soon, that same mundane-looking two-story house came into my mind, sharpened. I saw a street sign: Kilmuir Drive. I knew the area; it was in the Hilliard suburb a mile or so to the south of Tuttle Mall. A far nicer neighborhood than the one Kai lived in, the kind of 'burb young professionals with kids settled in because of the modest home prices, nice parks and good school system.

The kind of place an unleashed devil could do a whole lot of damage in a hurry if it had the chance.

I looked at Kai. "You wouldn't happen to have a gun around here, would you?"

He nodded. "Yeah, I got a nine under my bed. Ammo, too."

"Go get it. And put a shirt and some real shoes on." I pulled out my phone and started texting Mother Karen and Cooper to let them know where I was going. "Better get some food if you haven't eaten, because this could be a long night."

We got to Kilmuir Drive well after sundown. I slowed the car, scanning the houses, looking for the one from my vision. And there it was, sitting innocently in the middle of the block. Developers probably built it sometime in the late 80s; it was the kind of two-story, two-car garage place you could find in most any suburb in America. White aluminum siding. Picket fence. Red decorative shutters. Manicured lawn with a freshly-mulched flowerbed of chrysanthemums (white or yellow; I couldn't tell in the near darkness). The porch light was on, and a fluorescent glow from the kitchen illuminated the first-floor windows. Everything else was dark.

The more I stared at the entirely pleasant-looking place, the more dread I felt. Something was desperately wrong, but there was no physical sign of it. I blinked through to the ocularis view that would show me hidden magic and enchantments.

Wham!

"Shit!" The kick was to my eye socket this time, and I quickly blinked to a more mundane view.

"What's the matter?" Kai and Pal asked, nearly simultaneously.

"That's a heavy block. No tracking, no viewing. For all I know we'll get fried the moment we set foot on the porch." I pulled out my cell phone and dialed Riviera Jordan's number. It was only for emergencies, but this was starting to feel like one. Or it would be an emergency once we got inside.

The call went to her voicemail. I left her a quick message explaining the situation, and gave her the street address.

"Feel free to drop on by. Probably we'll need help. Thanks, and goodbye." I ended the call and shut off my ringer.

"I've never known you to willingly call for Circle assistance," Pal remarked. "Are you *sure* you're feeling all right?"

I'm pretty sure I don't feel like having my arm bitten off again, or getting my other eye burned out of my head, I thought back, irritated. *Besides, if something happens and she finds out I could have warned her but didn't, what do you think the odds are that she'll kick us out of Columbus?*

"Rather high," Pal admitted.

"Okay, so let's do this," I told Kai. "*Quietly.* Follow my lead. Keep your gun holstered until I tell you different."

He nodded, white-faced. "You're the boss."

Kai shouldered a black nylon backpack laden with rope, flashlights, kerosene, a first aid kit, and sundry tools. I retrieved my twelve gauge Mossberg 590 shotgun from the back seat. It was fully loaded with cartridges that contained eighteen pellets of mixed silver and iron buckshot: a little something for any sort of hostile creature I might encounter, magical or mundane. Ubiquemancy wasn't ideal for rapid attacks. I had done a few offensive spells often enough that I could get them to work with a fast phrase—"trip" and "shove" were good quickies, and I was still tweaking "zap" to change Pal—but killing words were considered one of the worst kinds of necromancy by pretty much everyone. As much trouble as I was in with the Regnum, I didn't want to make my situation any worse with serious darkside stuff.

We shut the Toyota's doors as quietly as possible and crept toward the front door, hoping none of the neighbors would see and call the cops. There were very few magical combat situations that mundane police forces couldn't make 200% worse.

Should we wait for Riviera to show up? I thought to Pal as we reached the cover of the front porch.

"I am quite concerned about this new-found prudence of yours," he replied.

No, seriously. Should we wait? Or will waiting get Kai's girl killed?

"Do we go in?" Kai whispered, his voice shaking.

"There's no guarantee that Riviera checks her voice mail promptly," Pal thought to me, "and I doubt any of her people are as effective at killing devils as you are. Our lack of apparent support may lull our opponent into a false sense of complacency."

He paused. "Or it could get us killed. One or the other."

Wow, you're a help, I thought to him.

I knew he meant his words to be encouraging, but they made me feel a little sick. Because, if I was honest with myself, I knew he was right…I was very, very good at killing devils. And I might have felt okay if my destructive talents had stopped there. But it seemed I was pretty good at killing damn near anything. Way better than I was at keeping people alive. My avoiding murder words had nothing to do with the Regnum's rules. It was because I really didn't need them.

I hated being good at something so fundamentally rotten. And I hated that I lived in a world where those particular skills came in so very handy. I wanted to be a good person, and I wasn't sure that was really possible once I got enough blood on my hands. Even if most of it was ichor. But I didn't feel right walking away from people in trouble, either, and I wasn't about to back down from a fight someone else started.

"Yes, we're going in," I replied, voice low. I leaned my shotgun against the white vinyl porch railing and pulled off my opera glove. Shoved it in the pocket of my jeans. I stared at the doorknob. "Odds are the house has some kind of protection, but maybe not. Pal, go to Kai, just in case."

He hopped over onto Kai's shoulder. I took a deep breath, and gently touched the front door knob with my flesh hand.

A hot blue bolt of magical electricity arced through me. My muscles spasmed painfully and I peed myself a little. And then I dropped like a sack of potatoes onto the Astroturfed porch boards.

Kai knelt beside me. "Are you okay?"

"Crap on a cracker, that hurt." I sat up, trying to shake the buzzing numbness out of my fingers. I didn't see any new lights coming on in the houses around, and nobody seemed to be peeking through blinds. "No surprise, though."

"What do we do?"

"Get insulated." I looked around. "You got a candy wrapper? Something made of plastic or wax paper?"

"Lemme check." He dug through his pockets and found a wadded-up cough drop wrapper. "Will this work?"

"It should. I only need it to work for a minute or two." Heck, I only *wanted* it to work for a minute or two. I held it in my hands and began my chant, quietly as I could, and as the old word began to summon magical forces, I felt a plasticky film start to shroud my skin.

Still chanting, I got to my feet, motioned for Kai to follow, and grabbed the doorknob. Locked. I switched up my chant and spoke an ancient word for "rust". The metal crumbled when I gave it a third hard twist.

And then we were standing in the dimness of the living room.

"Stay behind me," I whispered to Kai. Already I could feel the filminess disappearing. "I can see in the dark; try to leave your flashlight off."

Adrenaline surged in my bloodstream. Being pretty good at killing didn't mean I wouldn't get killed myself. I took a deep breath, blinked through to the night vision view, and stepped into the living room. My flesh eye only showed me the rough details of the dim room, but through my ocularis I saw a drip of blood spotting the pale carpet. The dark trail led to a door beneath the stairs.

You see that? I thought to Pal.

"The basement," he replied. "Of *course* it's in the basement."

We did a quick sweep of the first floor and upper floor, stepping as gently as possible to avoid squeaking the floorboards. Kai followed close behind me, quiet as a ghost. The rooms were mostly empty; what furniture was there seemed like the kind of stuff realtors placed to stage houses for sale. There were few signs that anybody was actually living there.

I went back to the basement door and tried the knob. No jolt. Not locked. I pushed, and it swung inward with a creak that seemed far too loud. Immediately, the stench of decaying flesh made my eyes water. The bloody drip continued down the carpeted stairs; it and the stairs ended at another door. I held my breath, listening. Nothing.

"What now?" Kai whispered, barely audible.

"We go down," I whispered back. "Get your nine out. Don't shoot me in the back."

His "okay" was an anxious exhalation, syllables swallowed by dread.

We descended.

At every careful step, I wondered if I should ease the basement door open or kick the thing in. If they didn't know we were there and weren't watching the door, a stealthy opening would give us an advantage. But if they knew we were coming, kicking it open might work better. Assuming the slam didn't startle someone into firing a weapon. Assuming they wouldn't just start firing at us whether they were startled or not. *Shit*. I hated this part.

Instinct took over when my hand was on the knob. I swung it open, fast and hard enough to bash anyone lurking on the other side. Nobody was.

I took in the whole scene in just a two heartbeats. The basement was unfinished and had no furniture or appliances besides the furnace unit in the corner. Someone had smeared a yards-wide complex necromancy diagram in the middle of the concrete floor with blood. It looked to be the kind of thing you made to open an extradimensional portal. To either side stood a pair of gangly figures in dark clothes; their faces had a shiny, unformed fetal look, and their arms and legs seemed just a bit too long for normal human proportions. A hairy naked middle-aged guy, blindfolded and ball-gagged, lay crucified in the middle of the diagram, his hands and feet staked to holes in the floor with rebar. I couldn't tell if he was still alive or not.

Above the crucified man stood a pretty blonde girl, maybe 18 or 19, also naked…and her eyes were the inflamed purple of the recently possessed. Alice, but not really. Not anymore.

And all around us were a dozen reanimated dead guys. The source of the terrible stench. Some of them were maybe just days dead, bloated and crawling with maggots, but others had been gone a long time, their desiccated flesh stretched and ragged over dry bones.

Not-Alice hissed and made a "Get them!" motion. The zombies lunged toward us with surprising speed; I had to admire the necromancy. The gangly figures pulled pistols from their waistbands but hung back, waiting.

Take 'em! I tossed Pal up in the air and spoke an ancient word to trigger my electroshock spell.

A tiny bright bolt of lightning sprang from my fingertip and hit him in the flank as he approached the apex of my throw. His fur went *poof!*—I'd worked the spell to steal the required energy from his hair. His tiny naked legs and tail windmilled in the air for the briefest moment. In the space between two of my own jackhammering heartbeats, his tail shrank, legs and body lengthened and thickened faster than gravity, and a new, thick pelt of heavy brown fur sprouted on his expanding hide.

His entire transformation took less than a second. When his paws landed on the concrete floor, he was no longer a slinky little ferret but a grizzly bear. 800 pounds of muscle and bone and righteous fury. He reared back, thunderously roared and took the head off the nearest rotter with a single paw-swipe.

I started blasting the zombies with my shotgun. Aimed for the neck and not the head. Decapitation's what stops zombies if the brains are already rotted away. The boom of my weapon made my ears ache. The air filled with a choking haze of smoke and stinking rot.

In seconds, my shotgun was empty. Kai had drawn his 9mm and was plugging away at the zombies still standing. Pal swiped the head off another of the creeps.

In the back, the ganglers were taking aim with their pistols. I dropped my spent shotgun and shouted an ancient word for "Shove!" as I pushed into the empty air. I felt the slam in my arms as my spell connected and they stumbled backward, their gun arms shoved to their sides.

This was my chance. I sprinted forward, sprang over the crucified guy and slapped not-Alice on her shoulder with my cold white hand. And dragged us both into my personal hell.

This was what remained of the nightmarish world my boyfriend Cooper had been enslaved in when he fell into a trap laid by a powerful pain-consuming devil called a Goad. It was a pocket dimension, an extradimensional space whose reality I controlled completely ever since I'd killed the Goad that had created it and rescued Cooper. The hellement became a permanent part of my magical landscape.

I'd tried to mask the evil of the place by turning it into a perfect replica of my childhood bedroom. Perpetual late afternoon sunlight streamed in through the mini-blinds, my stuffed animals lined up at attention on the dresser, my Buzz Lightyear comforter draped the bed. Beneath the pink dust ruffle, a thousand horrifying memories from the Goad's many victims slept in glass jars.

"What have you done? What is this place?" growled not-Alice, looking furious but a little uncertain. I'd managed to throw the creature for a loop. She appeared as a strange double-image now, the possessive devil visible as a kind of dark twin right behind her.

"You're in *my* house now." I reached under the bed, pulled out my longsword and pointed it at her. "Talk. What are you doing in Alice's body?"

"Useful. It has magic," the devil replied.

"For what?"

"To bring Mother here."

"And why does your mother want to be here?"

"Souls," the devil hissed wistfully. "So many delicious souls."

I sighed. That's all devils ever seemed to want. Human souls were apparently the popcorn shrimp of the spiritual world. I kept hoping a devil would tell me it was here for gambling, or to drink all the whiskey, download a bunch of porn, or steal the secret recipe for Coca-Cola. No such luck. It was all souls, all the time.

"Let Alice go and I'll be as nice as I possibly can," I said.

The devil shrieked and lunged at me. I spun aside like a matador and grabbed the darkness clinging to Alice with my left hand. She/it fought me, clawing at my arms, but I held on, wrestled them both down to the floor.

Ignoring the stinging blows she was landing on my face, I tightened my grip and yanked as hard as I could. The darkness ripped clean away from her with a scream that could have shattered glass. Alice tumbled forward, jerking in the throes of a seizure. I was left gripping a dark squirming mass that reminded me of an enormous liver fluke.

"I get it. You're still just a baby and you don't understand," I told it as it struggled to break free. It was clammy, frigid through and through. Devils tend to be creatures of heat or cold. I was glad that this one was cold, because I worked better with fire.

"This is *my* place." I stared at the wall and willed a blast furnace into existence. Mount Doom didn't burn half as hot. "I don't *need* to do magic here. This *is* my magic."

I flung the boneless devil into the boiling metal. The thing writhed, shrieking and jerking and steaming. It tried to haul itself out of the inferno but I slammed the grate on it. The furnace shook as it struggled, but I held fast. Through the bars I watched it burn. Watched it die. When I was satisfied it was nothing but ash, I erased the furnace and knelt beside Alice to see how she was doing.

She was pale, breathing shallowly. Clearly suffering from shock. Exorcisms take time for a reason. It's a trauma to your system to have another entity take over your mind and body…but it's even worse to have that control suddenly torn away.

"You're lucky you didn't stroke out and die." I brushed a sweaty strand of hair out of one of her wide-staring blue eyes. She really was lovely; I could see why Kai had fallen for her. A tiny little thing, thin and pale and maybe just over five feet tall. So vulnerable, especially here in my hell. I could do whatever I wanted in here. I could tie her down and slowly pull her guts out and listen to her scream....

"Jesus!" I jerked back, suddenly aware of how hideous my thoughts had turned.

Not my thoughts. Those can't be my thoughts. I stared around at the room; suddenly all the replicas of my toys seemed to be silently mocking me.

Magic always had a cost. And the cost to me in this place was my humanity and sanity. I couldn't stay or I'd become just like the devils I'd killed.

I quickly gathered up Alice, carried her to the big red portal door in the corner, and took us back to the real world.

When we rematerialized in the basement, I saw that Pal in his grizzly form had decapitated the remaining zombies and mauled the ganglers. The uncanny pair lay in pieces scattered across the concrete, molasses-thick ichor pooling around their torn limbs. Definitely not human.

"What are they?" I asked Pal.

"Some kind of sidhe, I think. Hired minions, regardless."

Kai hurried over, sweaty and spattered with blood and ichor. "Oh God, is she okay?"

At the sound of his voice, Alice's eyes fluttered, and she began coughing and gagging. I quickly set her down on the concrete and turned her head to the side. She started vomiting up the dead hatchling. It looked much as it had in my hell, though thankfully it was much smaller.

"Oh, god!" Kai looked like he might start puking himself.

"She needs a healer," I told him. "But at least she's alive."

"So does this fellow." Pal was peering down at the crucified man. "I think he's one of the Governing Circle agents. I think I remember seeing him at the meeting we had with Riviera."

"He's still alive? Wow." I pulled out my cell phone. No service.

"Guys, I'm going upstairs to call Mother Karen," I told them. "She'll know what to do."

79

I ran up the stairs, out of the house onto the front lawn and had just lifted my phone to my ear when the wind kicked up and I heard an ominous rumbling.

Oh, shit.

The sky opened, a bright lightning gash in the black firmament, and a creature that looked like an enormous crystalline replica of some alien solar system cruised through. A vast cloud of fiery plasma in which a dozen jewel organs circled a glowing magma heart. A Virtus, one of the prime enforcer spirits of the Virtus Regnum.

I stood there very still, feeling like an inchworm seeing the sole of a giant boot coming down. At first I felt nothing but gut-churning terror: I was so, *so* dead. So incredibly dead. And so were my friends, if the Virtus spotted them. I prayed Kai would stay put in the basement.

But then I felt hope: maybe if I did some first-class fast talking, it would leave Kai and Pal and Alice alone? Then came a squelch of despair: mercy was not part of the Regnum's program, and I damn well knew that. I was the worst kind of idiot to think for even a moment that it might care the teensiest, most miniscule bit that I'd just stopped an invasion of soul-devouring devils. This creature only respected the letter of the law, and the rulebook wasn't on my side.

And that's when frustration and anger started skipping in circles through my mind. Goddammit, I'd been *so close* to making things right here—why did the Virtus have to show up and screw up everything? Dammit. Dammit, dammit, *dammit*!

I mightily resisted the urge to scream and flip double birds at the spirit in the sky. And that moment of self-restraint was a mistake. I'd let my adrenaline ebb just a little, and suddenly complete exhaustion flooded through me, suffocating my rage and will to fight and everything else. My bones suddenly felt like they'd turned to concrete. I was completely beat. And probably the Virtus knew it.

Its icy diamond eyes fixed on me, beholding me like an exterminator sizing up a fire ant nest. It had probably been shadowing me for a long time. Probably it had hoped that the devil would do its job for it and it wouldn't have to bother with killing me itself.

"You have disobeyed the law," it boomed. The ground shook. "You have violated the prohibition against grand necromancy. You have murdered. You shall be destroyed."

I'd heard it all before, but this time, I didn't have the power to defend myself. When I killed my first Virtus, I'd been flush with the magical energy of a very powerful devil. And frankly I'd had more than my share of blind shithouse luck that day. I couldn't jump up and drag this new Virtus into my hell, and even if I did, I wasn't sure the power I wielded there would be enough. And I couldn't run back into the house; the Virtus would just burn it all to ashes and consider it a job cleanly done.

So I did the only thing that seemed reasonable to my exhausted self: I fell to my knees on the grass, shut my eyes, and waited to die.

"Stop!" I heard a woman shout.

I opened my eyes. Riviera Jordan stood by the curb, looking fashionably stern in a dark designer suit a lawyer might wear to some big trial, backlit in the headlights of a big grey SUV, her short silver hair a bright halo around her face.

"I have authority here!" She held up an ivory tablet inscribed with some kind of ancient runes. "You may not harm Miss Shimmer. She's under my protection. Leave now!"

The Virtus glowered at Riviera. "If you deny me my duty, we will not return to Columbus. Your city will be without the protection of the Virtus Regnum. Do you truly want that?"

"I think we need her more than we need you," Riviera drawled in her upper-crust Southern accent. "And you lot weren't doing much to protect us anyhow."

"Insolence," the Virtus grumbled, but it disappeared back into the night sky, the lightning gash sealing behind it, leaving behind only the smell of ozone and a faintly glowing ring of smoke in the air.

I slowly climbed to my feet. "Two people in the basement need a healer. One is your guy. They were gonna use him as a sacrifice in a portal opening ritual. He's in bad shape."

"Devil or necromancer?" Riviera asked.

"Devil." I stretched, and my spine popped.

"You kill it?" She pulled a pack of Marlboros from her suit jacket and tapped out a cigarette.

"Yes, ma'am!"

"Good girl."

Riviera turned her head to call over her shoulder: "Rafé, Loretta, grab your kits and head down to the basement!"

Two Circle agents in dark suits with red cross armbands and white canvas shoulder bags piled out of the back of the SUV and hurried into the house.

"Thank you," I said to Riviera. "I guess this means Pal and I get to stay in Columbus?"

She smiled and lit her cigarette. "Just don't make me regret this."

The Porcupine Boy

Eddie Bellweather got out of his Honda Odyssey with his satchel, locked the door and grinned at the glossy new graphics he'd gotten his buddy Rafael to paint on the van's side. The logo bore the words *PORCUPINE BOY PATIENT SERVICES* in a blue circle around a cute cartoon porcupine in a Superman-style caped crusader costume with a fists-on-hips pose, a red PB on his chest shield in place of Supe's stylized "S". Rafael had promised him that DC couldn't sue him over his new mascot, and it was exactly what Eddie had envisioned. It was bold and friendly, and Eddie figured it perfectly conveyed the little-guy heroism he'd striven for when he started his business. People were counting on him. He was *needed*. And that was something he'd grown up thinking could never happen.

"It is a *great* day to be alive." He booped his mascot's flat black nose with his index finger and then headed up the tree-shaded walkway to Dr. Shanahan's office.

He hadn't set foot in this particular office in at least three years, and remembered it as having a cozy, unassuming waiting room with office furniture from the 80s. The staff always decorated for the holidays, and this time of year, the walls would be covered in cardboard cutouts of cutely menacing mummies, black cats, little-girl witches and pumpkins. Eddie thought those kinds of decorations were hopelessly cheesy when he was a teenager, but he'd come to appreciate their whimsy as he got older.

Only one of his clients was a patient here—old Miss Dorotka—and Dr. Shanahan was fine with renewing her prescriptions without making her take the stressful trek to his exam table. Until now, for whatever reason. Eddie was confident he could get it sorted out.

But when he pushed through the glass doors, instead of the outdated chairs, plastic-framed public health posters and dollar store Halloween décor, he saw fancy new seating, potted plants and expensive-looking oil paintings. And, on one wall, an ostentatiously large crucifix of a sheet-pale Christ nailed to a mahogany cross. It certainly wasn't there before. The sight of it made Eddie's stomach tighten.

He didn't have anything against Christianity, not exactly. Not *officially*. But the cross was the kind of thing his mother would have put up on the living room, not as a reminder of any of the things that Jesus lived and died for, but as a stern notice to all visitors (and particularly Eddie's few friends) that This Is a Christian House And We Don't Tolerate That Kind of Thing Here. Her version of Christianity had little to do with goodwill towards humankind or turning the other cheek and everything to do with shame and fronting piety.

Eddie had plenty of Christian clients who weren't bent the way his mother was; they were good folks of faith. He had no reason to think that the owner of this cross should be less like them and more like his mother. But he *also* had clients who were Jewish, Muslim, Buddhist, or atheist, and a huge, hard-to-miss cross like this was likely to make them feel a bit unwelcome. So many Christians had done so many terrible things in the name of that crucifix: The Inquisition, the Crusades, the Magdalene Laundries. Dr. Shanahan seemed like the kind of man who'd cracked enough history books to realize that, and who just on basic principle would want to avoid alienating patients for no reason. So what was going on here?

If Eddie was being honest with himself, the cross gave him a twinge of envy. What must it be like to so firmly believe in a higher power, to have faith in the existence of a grand supernatural order that transcended the mundane bullshit that made up so much of everyday human existence? Eddie wanted to believe; he *craved* belief, at times. But he was fundamentally a man who could only believe in what he could see, taste, or touch. Even the powerful hallucinogens that his friends swore would open his inner eye to the wonders hidden beyond the limitations of fleshly senses left him queasy and agnostic. Eddie figured that the right thing to do was the right thing to do regardless of whether God existed to give you wings for it or not. But some days, he'd have nearly been willing to give his right nut for proof that there was more to the world than met his eye.

Eddie turned away from the cross and focused on the check-in counter. The receptionist during his previous visits had been a plump older lady who reminded him of his great aunt Judy, the one person in his family who never treated him like a loser. But now, the receptionist was an extremely pretty woman in her mid-20s who looked like she should be in a toothpaste commercial.

She gave him a frosty white smile. "May I help you?"

"Hi, I'm Eddie with Porcupine Boy Patient Services," he replied. "I'm helping one of Dr. Shanahan's long-term patients, Dorotka Nowak. I tried to get her maintenance meds refilled at the pharmacy, but they said they couldn't get this office to fax in a new script. So I'm here to check on that."

Her eyes narrowed suspiciously. "What's your relation to Mrs. Nowak?"

"As I said, I'm with Porcupine Boy. I'm here in my capacity as her patient advocate." He opened his satchel, pulled out the medical power of attorney form Miss Dorotka signed and showed it to the receptionist.

"Let me bring up her file." She turned to the computer and started keying in a query. "Porcupine Boy is kind of a weird name for a company, don't you think?"

Eddie's smile didn't waver. "My great-grandfather was Zuni. In his religion, porcupines symbolize the power of faith and trust, both of which are critical for patient advocacy."

He tapped the logo on his polo shirt. "And the 'Boy' part represents the idea that I'm getting out there and fighting for my clients like Beast Boy, or Astro Boy."

Eddie hadn't told her any lies, but none of those were the reason he got the nickname Porcupine Boy back in the day. When he was 16, his parents kicked him out of their trailer for going to the movies with a black girl and he ended up living in a downtown Granite City flop with a bunch of crust punks. One night, he watched a torrent of "Hellraiser" on a stolen laptop while he got blitzed on meth and cheap gin. He ended up shoving 100 sewing needles into his forehead, cheeks, and arms before he passed out. His flopmates found him a couple of hours later, and one of the older guys in the house—who'd never seen the movie and didn't know what a cenobite was—started calling him "Porcupine Boy".

The nickname stuck harder than the needles. Even though it was a misunderstanding, Eddie felt like getting a real nickname was a sign he'd been accepted into the local punk community and wasn't just another gangly white trash throwaway nobody gave a shit about. So he just rolled with it, and when he scraped together a few hundred dollars he got a huge tattoo of a porcupine on his chest along with his nickname in black gothic lettering.

It didn't matter to Eddie that not everybody understood or cared about his personal brand. What mattered was that *he* knew what it meant, and he'd been able to change the meaning of his nickname to adapt to who he had become as a person in the decade since.

"Huh," said the receptionist. "Looks like she's never actually seen Dr. Shanahan. She'll need to come in for an exam before he can write her a prescription."

"What do you mean she's never seen Dr. Shanahan?" Eddie blinked at her. "I brought her in myself right after she became my client."

"Oh, well, she probably saw Dr. Shanahan's uncle. He owned the practice before, but Dr. Shanahan bought it from him last year when the old guy got pancreatic cancer."

Shit. Eddie's stomach dropped. Not that any cancer was a day at the beach, but pancreatic cancer was particularly brutal. Dr. Shanahan seemed like a thoroughly decent guy and didn't deserve a terrible disease like that. "I sure am sorry to hear that…how's he doing?"

"I think he died?" The receptionist shrugged indifferently, and Eddie decided he didn't like her very much regardless of how pretty she was. "I never met him, so I don't know. Anyway, your client's going to need to make an appointment."

"Are you sure that's really necessary? She's very elderly, and her immune system is compromised. Getting out to appointments is hazardous for her. She's been doing telemedicine for urgent care, and she's got a USB blood pressure monitor and such. I'm a registered nurse, so I can do a blood draw if the doctor wants labs done. Can we arrange for a remote exam instead?" He hadn't drawn Miss Dorotka's blood before, but he'd done that for other clients and there hadn't ever been a problem with the doctors or the labs.

The receptionist looked bored and a little irritated. "She'll have to see the doctor in person if she wants to be a patient here."

Eddie tried to swallow down his growing frustration. There was no point to making the old lady come in. She was frail but stable and in pretty good health considering her advanced age…but that depended on her getting her medications. Particularly the ferropentin, which she had to take for recurring fevers she'd suffered ever since she'd gone on an archaeological dig in Egypt when she was a young woman. It was some kind of parasitic infection in her blood that couldn't be cured; she'd described it as being like malaria. Eddie hadn't gotten a lot of information about whatever the pathogen was, but the important details as far as he was concerned were that she wasn't contagious, and the ferropentin was critical for her well-being. Without it, she got moody and started suffering memory problems. Her mobility took a serious hit, and her immune problems worsened. One of the worst symptoms was a terrible, ulcerated rash on her skin; out of self-consciousness she'd start wearing long sleeves, gloves, and a veil. She denied feeling pain, but Eddie didn't believe that for one second; she walked like every step was on broken glass.

He was sorely tempted to tell the receptionist that they'd just find another doctor…but he also knew there was no way he could find one before Miss Dorotka's medication situation was dire. "Could I speak to Dr. Shanahan about that?"

"He's in with a patient. You can leave a message for him and he'll get back to you later, but I promise it's standard office policy and he'll tell you exactly what I did."

Eddie took a deep breath and forced his smile. Reminded himself that if interactions with medical offices were easy and logical, nobody would need to hire him for anything. "Ok, well, she's almost out of her medication. She'll be in a bad way in a day or two. How soon can I bring her in?"

Miss Dorotka lived in a late-1800s Victorian up in Polish Hills. The neighborhood had begun as a blue-collar immigrant enclave—her place originally housed several families—but gentrified in the 1960s and became a favorite of Ford and Buick executives before their auto plants moved to Mexico. Now, many of the once-grand houses on her street were boarded up. Both her neighbors had abandoned their homes and mortgages years before. The old lady's physical isolation worried her great-niece Krystyna, who'd found Eddie in the Yellow Pages and contracted with him to check on her every few days.

Krystyna was an enigma, through and through, and during his occasional bouts of insomnia he found himself thinking about her. Wondering. They'd met just once at a coffee shop to discuss Miss Dorotka's situation. She was ash-blonde, athletically slim, looked to be in her late 20s but carried herself like she was the 40-something

CEO of a megacorporation. Not arrogant, but someone who was in control, wise to everything happening around her. But despite her expensive clothes, she wore an old-fashioned wristwatch and carried an older flip phone instead of a smartphone. She had the faintest Polish accent, and wore all black in a way that probably just came across as very put-together and professional to most people, but he could smell the clove cigarettes on her clothes. Djarum Blacks.

And *that* familiar smell always made him nostalgic for the times he'd ended up at the local goth club. He'd liked the music okay, but there was something mystical about the scene that attracted him even though he knew that his sunny punk self could never fit into it. There, in the dark under the blacklights surrounded by strangers in black lace and shiny black vinyl, the air filled with clove smoke, it felt like more was possible than met his eye. Something strange, something supernatural.

There was far more to Krystyna than met his eye, he was certain. If America had a throne, she'd belong upon it. On those late nights when his imagination got the better of him, he wondered if she was a hotshot business woman by day and a gothic domme by night. Breaking ordinary men with ropes and violet wands to turn them into something extraordinary. Not that he could ever find out. She'd never be into a guy like him, but knowing he was doing something to help her made him feel that he was in service to something greater than himself.

Eddie parked at the foot of Miss Dorotka's steep driveway walked up the blacktop to her house, stooping every few feet to collect bundled newspapers. He hadn't been able to get her on the phone when he was at the doctor's office, but that wasn't so unusual. The neglected papers worried him, though. One of her favorite activities was doing the daily crossword while she drank her morning coffee, so he suspected that either walking down the concrete steps hurt too much, or she was too mentally foggy to work the puzzles now.

The front door wasn't locked. He opened it a crack and called inside, "Miss Dorotka? It's Eddie. Are you okay in there?"

He heard a muffled "Yes" followed by something in Polish. Something wasn't right, and his stomach churned at all the dire imaginations crowding into his brain. Perhaps she'd fallen and shattered her leg and was struggling to shove the broken bone back into place in the living room. Or maybe she'd spilled boiling water on herself in the kitchen trying to make her tea. But he pushed all those grim thoughts away: it was a great day to be alive, and she was alive, and that was most important.

"I'm coming inside, okay?" He stepped through the door and pulled it shut behind him. The foyer looked as it had four days ago: mail piled on the dark wood console table, boots and shoes rowed neatly in plastic trays on the scarred hardwood floor. The house was eerily quiet compared to his other clients' homes, where infomercials and FOX News blasted so loudly day and night he could barely think. Miss Dorotka didn't own a television or a computer or even a radio, preferring to listen to old LPs and read even older books. Her rotary phone was an ancient, solid hunk of Bakelite built to survive a nuclear war.

Though everything looked to be in order, the air carried a sour, spoiled odor—probably the garbage needed to go out. But there was something else, a carnal rot like long-spoiled meat, and another stink that reminded him of when the old flop got a nightmarish roach problem. The memory of wandering bleary into the bathroom, flipping on the light and seeing the walls blackened by the skittering little monsters made his skin goosepimple unpleasantly. He hoped the old lady didn't have some kind of infestation because then whoever did pest control would have to spread poison everywhere and it wouldn't be any good for her health. One of his patients got Parkinson's after exterminators fumigated her place for fleas. Not that cockroaches were any better for Miss Dorotka's health, either; salmonella would kill her a lot faster than low-grade nerve poisoning. A gross situation either way. He hoped his nose was mistaken.

He found Miss Dorotka standing in the middle of her living room with her back to the doorway. She wore a long-sleeved black dress and a heavy funeral veil and stood so still that he wasn't sure she hadn't just dressed a mannequin and set it to stand watch in the room.

"Miss Dorotka?" he asked.

The figure stirred and turned her head toward him. "Oh, Eddie, so nice to see you."

Her voice was strangely distorted, hoarse and dry. She didn't sound like herself at all. How could she have gotten so bad in just a few days?

"I went to the doctor's office to see about your prescription," he said. "Bad news is, they won't renew your script without an appointment. Good news is, I got you one for this afternoon. But we need to leave soon."

"I don't want to go outside." She swayed back and forth as if she were suspended from invisible wires. "I don't want to be seen like this."

"I know you don't." Eddie felt a fresh pang of frustration. "I tried, I really did, but Doctor Shanahan's nephew is running the office now, and apparently he's kind of a hard-ass about things."

"Do we really need a doctor? My medication doesn't hurt anyone. All they need is a slip of paper with a signature on it, yes?"

Eddie felt a guilty heat rise in his face. He could forge a script; that was one of the many illicit skills he'd honed back in the old days. He knew all the local pharmacies that didn't bother checking too closely. Hell, he still had an old prescription pad from a defunct office hidden in a pocket of his satchel.

"I'm not allowed to write prescriptions," he said. "I know some nurses can, but I can't. I think it's best if we try to keep everything on the up-and-up, ma'am. But if you really don't feel you can go out, though, we can try something different."

It was a slippery slope, he warned himself. If he broke the rules for Miss Dorotka, he'd almost certainly get away with it. And then he'd break rules for other clients, and he'd fall back into his old habits. The rules he broke would get bigger and bigger until one day he'd get arrested again, and he'd lose everything he'd worked so hard to build. The new, heroic Porcupine Boy would once again be nothing more than a broken idiot who drunkenly shoved needles in his own face. That future loomed so clear and terrible in his mind that even if forging a script for her was purely a matter of kindness and efficiency…he couldn't justify it. Other patients depended on him, too.

She gave a heavy, rasping sigh, dry as a desert wind. "I do not want a nice boy like you to get in trouble. I will go to the appointment. But I need to find my things…."

He found her misplaced purse, aluminum walking cane and state ID—she hadn't been able to drive in many years—and then gripped her bony elbow and helped her totter out of the house and down the blacktop to his van. Once she was out in the light, Eddie realized that she was wearing a surgical mask under the heavy veil; he could barely see her eyes as shadowed caves beneath her painted-on eyebrows, and he couldn't see her mouth and nose at all beneath the green mask. The unpleasant smells that had worried him in the house clung to her strongly, and the light breeze did nothing to diffuse them. He first wondered if she'd spilled garbage on her clothes, but the dress looked clean enough. And then he worried that perhaps she had a wound or bed sore that had gone seriously bad. Nasty anaerobic bacteria *could* give off odors like these. And if that was the case, it was definitely for the best that they were going to the doctor.

"You should make sure to keep your doors locked," he said as he pulled out into the street. "I'm pretty sure junkies are squatting in the abandoned houses around here, and any of them could just stroll right in."

"I don't mind company," she replied lightly, shading her already deeply-shadowed eyes with a gloved hand. "They are welcome to stroll in if they like. I would make them tea."

Eddie paused, wondering if this was the fever talking, or if she were making a little joke. "These guys could really hurt you, ma'am."

He remembered all the shameful times he'd been high and threw rocks at people leaving snooty dinner clubs or broke uptown windows or started fights with prep school jocks just because his amphetamine-stoked anger at the world made it seem like the fun thing to do. Not just fun; it felt *justified*. There were so many rotten people living nice lives that they didn't deserve. So many rich people who'd rigged the system in their favor so that the heirlooms they stole and the families they ruined were just ledger entries to be handled by their accountants. Miss Dorotka was nothing like the spoiled plutocrats he'd hated when he was young and full of meth and Marxism…but anyone who had a house looked rich to someone homeless.

"They might not mean to," he said. "They might mean to but feel terrible about it once they sober up. But they could really, really hurt you."

She laughed, a dry rasp. "You speak as if I am but a girl, as if I haven't had to deal with violent young men my whole life. As if I never saw the treads of German tanks crush my neighbors' bodies into the cold winter mud."

Suddenly he felt acutely embarrassed. How could he have forgotten all that she'd gone through? Krystyna hadn't gone into a lot of details, but the whole *Hey, my great aunt survived the Nazis and went all over the Middle East on expeditions like Indiana Jones* should have been something he could keep in his mind. "I'm sorry, ma'am, I didn't mean to sound condescending. I'm just worried for you, that's all."

She patted his knee. Her hand felt like sticks inside the white cotton glove. "And I am touched by your concern. But I understand the addict's mind and I have no fear of it."

Her remark puzzled Eddie a little. What did she know about addiction? If she truly understood it the way he did, she *should* be afraid. But if he asked questions, he might only manage to stick his foot further down his throat. It was more important to him that she see him as an educated guy with a brain in his head.

So he drove in silence, and she dozed beneath her veil, and soon they arrived back at Dr. Shanahan's office. The waiting room was empty, and the white-toothed receptionist sat playing Candy Crush on her phone behind the counter. After Eddie got her attention, she quickly checked Miss Dorotka in and escorted them to a small exam room in the back.

"Do you want me to stay with you?" Eddie asked as he helped her onto the exam table. It was awkward with him being a man, but some patients liked having someone they knew in the room the first time they met with an unfamiliar doctor.

"I will be fine," she said. "I will call if I need you."

So Eddie went back out to the waiting room, settled in a chair closest to the exam rooms, and started reading a copy of *National Geographic*. He'd just gotten engrossed in an article about the Saqqara necropolis in Egypt when he heard raised voices.

"*Do diabła z tob !*" Miss Dorotka shouted.

Oh, crap. If she was swearing in Polish, shit was getting real back there. Eddie dropped his magazine and sprinted to the exam room, the receptionist close behind him.

He pushed through the door...and he stopped dead in the doorway, stunned into a scared-deer freeze at the mind-breaking impossibility of the scene before him. His brain flat rejected what his eyes beheld. The receptionist pushed past him, then gave a strangled gasp and stood stock-still, her cell phone clattering to the grey parquet floor.

His brain started to assemble the impossible visual pieces. Miss Dorotka stood very tall in the middle of the room. She'd pushed her veil back and pulled her surgical mask down. She had no eyes, no mouth, no nose. Just holes like bottomless tombs carved into desert rocks. He'd seen coke addicts whose noses had rotted off, and her face didn't look like that. They were dark as collapsed stars, ragged bloodless skin opening into a vast empty void where flesh and bone should have been.

But *something* was spilling out of the dark *nothing*. Wriggling legless things like eels. Gleaming black and segmented like poisonous centipedes, or scorpions. Eddie's nose caught the sour insectoid stench from the house, and his skin shivered with goosebumps.

They were pouring out in dozens and dozens, cascading onto the doctor who had fallen to his knees at her feet. The strange vermin burrowing into his ears and eyes, filling his nose and mouth so he couldn't take a breath to make any noise louder than a strained grunting. The doctor clawed at his swarmed face, and the wrigglers burrowed into his flesh, stripping his hands and head skeletal in seconds.

The receptionist swore under her breath and out of the corner of his eye he saw her step back, try to flee, but the shiny wriggling dark swarmed over the floor and up her legs, and she didn't have time to make another sound before they were all over her face like iron filings on a magnet, clogging her nose and throat, the air filled with the papery rasp of hundreds of tiny maws devouring clothes and meat and bones.

This could not be. It *could not* be, but it was, and Eddie held his breath, waiting with clenched, sweating dread for the wrigglers to attack him, too…but they did not.

In fifty heartbeats, there was nothing left of the doctor but a pile of pens, pocket change, a belt buckle, the metal parts of a stethoscope, and his shoes. Nothing remained of the receptionist—whose name he belatedly realized he never even knew—except her shoes and her cell phone.

The mass of voracious vermin wriggled back to Miss Dorotka, swarmed up to her face and disappeared back into a mouth that was no longer a void hole but an actual mouth with soft pink lips and straight pearly teeth —

Eddie blinked. Old Miss Dorotka was now young Krystyna, lovely and mysterious as he remembered. She gazed at him gravely, her expression a mix of sadness and resignation.

"I am sorry this happened." She smoothed the front of the black dress and put her veil back into place. "And I am even sorrier you had to see it."

Eddie's mind still couldn't fully process what he'd just witnessed. A part of him was utterly horrified and wanted to run screaming…but another, greater part of him was shivering with awe. This woman—was she really a woman?—was proof of the grand supernatural. She was proof that there was some greater power lurking in the seams of the universe. She was a tantalizing hint that he could find proof for all the eldritch things he'd heard rumors of.

Feeling dizzy and disconnected from his own body, Eddie stared down into the receptionist's shoes. They were perfectly empty.

"There's no blood," he blurted dumbly.

"The hungry host is thorough," she replied, a faint smile playing on her lips. "But it does not care for vinyl or steel. There will be no DNA, no evidence. If the police look for clues, it will be as if these people simply vanished."

"There could be hidden cameras," Eddie found himself saying. "They're not supposed to put them in exam rooms. It's a huge HIPAA violation. But some doctors are paranoid. Or pervs. Let me check."

He pulled on a pair of nitrile gloves from the box on the counter and started giving the room a thorough once-over, shining his cell phone flashlight around to try to catch the gleam of hidden lenses. More than anything, it was something practical to do while his mind settled. Two people were dead. *Murdered*, if she had any sort of conscious control over the hideous little monsters that had come out of her. But if there was no video—and he wasn't finding any cameras—then what would he say to the police even if he wanted to report what had happened? If he ran away, she could probably just track him down. He had no idea what she was capable of. If he ran away, he'd never know her secrets.

"You are helping me?" Krystyna sounded incredulous.

Act normal, he told himself.

"You're…you're still my client," he said. "Protecting you from possible medical privacy violations is literally my job."

He ducked out into the hall to check the walls and ceiling and found nothing. "We should leave, ma'am, before anyone else comes."

Eddie plucked the check-in sheet that the receptionist hadn't yet processed off her desk, folded it, and stuck it in his back pocket. He'd burn it later.

His mind still turning the situation over and over like a Rubik's Cube he wasn't smart enough to solve, he escorted her out of the office, down the walk and put her in the passenger seat of his van.

As he was backing out of the space, the whole purpose of the visit came back to him. "Oh, crap. Your medication. I guess I'll just forge you a script."

"Well, I don't need it *now*," she replied. "I won't need it for…months. I hope. I'll start aging visibly, first. Then the fevers will come on. And then the rest of the unpleasantness."

Sighing, she pulled off the cotton gloves and removed the veil. "I didn't mean for this to happen. I thought that if I saw the doctor I could control it, but he was just so very unpleasant. The hunger was greater than my goodwill could bear."

"Were…were you born this way?" He pulled out onto the main road.

"Oh, no. I was born a perfectly ordinary child in Żoliborz in 1885. In 1903 I met a visiting British student named James Shruberry who was studying archaeology at the University of Warsaw. We married in 1907, and in 1910 I accompanied him on a dig in Egypt. The expedition leader thought he'd discovered the tomb of a pharaoh, full of untold mysteries and riches; it was, unfortunately, the tomb of a priest of Nyarlathotep."

She paused, rubbing her forehead as if she had a headache. "The black wind rose and each of us saw the god in a different form. It appeared as an indescribable monstrosity to my husband and the other scientists, and the experience utterly broke their minds. My husband died in a sanitarium right before the Great War.

"But the god appeared to me as a thin man seemingly carved from alabaster. And he told me he would give me a gift: eternal life. But of course it came at a dire cost."

"You have to kill to stay alive?" Eddie asked.

"No, I will live until the end of the universe. Even if they caught me and electrocuted me, if they drew and quartered me and burned me down to ashes, it would make no difference." She sounded supremely frustrated.

"The Nazis did that—burned me in the ovens without even knowing I'd destroyed fifty of them. The host emerged from their hellish plane and stitched my particles back together. I live, period. I must kill to stay *young*, to stay *beautiful*, to stay *sane*. And if I do not kill, the madness and disease overtakes me…and people die. And then I must live with the knowledge of what I've done."

"That sounds awful," Eddie replied.

"It simply *is*. I hoped this time that I could stave off the inevitable with the medication, but alas."

"Have you ever tried to lock yourself away? I mean, more than you have now."

She gave a short, bitter laugh. "Oh, of course I have. Many, many times. Somehow, I am always found. Often by a child. It's distressing."

"Why don't you kill people who need killing, then?" Eddie didn't like saying that out loud, but it was true: some folks were beyond redemption. And everybody had to die sooner or later.

"I don't know who needs killing," she protested. "I don't have the power to see into a man's soul!"

"What about the fifty Nazis you killed?"

"Nazis are purely rotten. One cannot regret killing a Nazi. But the rest of the world rallied together and annihilated them, as well they should have. I might as well wish to kill dodos."

Eddie blinked. "Do…do you not watch the news?"

"I haven't had a TV in years. Too many ads, too much hype. It's tiresome."

"What about the Internet?"

"I have heard it's for pornography." She shook her head. "I do not care for that."

"Well, I feel weird being the one to tell you this, but there are a lot of Nazis around these days. And skinheads, and Klan members…and maybe some of them are just dumb young guys, but plenty are grade-A scumbags."

"Really?" She looked startled. "I am frankly astonished that they exist in this enlightened age in such an advanced country."

"They've always been around, hiding like roaches," he replied, sneaking sideways glances at her to gauge her reaction. "It's just they've gotten bolder recently. All those message boards and online echo chambers to get each other fired up. They feel…justified."

The old shame washed through him again. He signaled left and turned onto her street.

"Their great-grandfathers would have fought the original Nazis." Krystyna twisted the gloves in her lap and gazed out the window. "The universe's dark humor never ceases to surprise me."

She paused, biting her lower lip thoughtfully. "So you can help me find some, when the time comes?"

"Oh, sure. I used to fight them all the time at punk clubs. I know where they hang out."

"Astonishing." She shook her head again.

Eddie shifted in his seat, shivering a little as he imagined the shiny black wrigglers spilling from her hollowed-out head again. "I had a question. When I came to your house this morning…would the host have eaten me?"

She laughed with genuine merriment, and the sparkling sound thrilled him. "Oh, no. I chose you over all the other nurses and home health aides for a reason. You've marked yourself, so you're perfectly safe."

He side-eyed her as he pulled up into her driveway. "Marked myself? How do you mean?"

"The porcupine! You have a tattoo, yes? The host fears the porcupine spirit —I don't entirely know why, but I suppose everything has a nemesis."

"That's good to know." He smiled as he parked and turned off the van.

As they got out and stood stretching on the warm blacktop, he did some quick math in his head. "So you've been around for…134 years?"

It was over 100 years longer than he'd been alive. The age gap was as daunting as the Grand Canyon or the whole Atlantic Ocean. And yet he couldn't help but try to imagine ways to bridge it.

She blinked at him in the sunlight as if she hadn't considered her own age in quite some time. "That sounds right."

"So you've learned a thing or two, I'm guessing?"

Her expression darkened and she looked away. "Clearly I know a bit less than I thought."

He tried to think how to phrase his question as he walked her to the front door. "I mean…you know about the occult? You know about what's really possible, and what isn't?"

She smiled. "Yes, *that* I know a little something about."

"Would you teach me?" he blurted out. "I…I could take you out to dinner. Off the clock. Maybe we could go dancing. You probably know ballroom way better than I do, but if you don't, we could both learn —"

"Eddie." She turned and touched his cheek with a warm, soft hand. Her gaze was level and sad. "I will outlive you. By a very long time. I cannot have children. I would make you an accessory to many, many murders."

"I know. But, I mean…for you, I'm safe…no one in the history of my entire life has gotten attached to me. Not ever." The admission made a hot blush bloom in his cheeks and nearly made tears rise in his eyes, so he forced himself to smile. "But it's a great day to be alive, and so why not live? Why lock yourself away? You have so much more to offer the world than just killing a few Nazis every year. I'm *sure* of it."

As he said the words, he realized he believed every single one of them. Perhaps this was his truest calling: helping this woman who was so thoroughly cursed discover ways to use that dark power to aid humanity. And maybe he couldn't succeed in the face of so much primeval horror, but he felt deep in his heart that the *trying* mattered. The right thing to do was still the right thing to do whether he'd be remembered for it or not.

She gave him a crooked smile. "You're a strangely convincing man."

He grinned back. "So, dinner? Dancing? Maybe a trip to look at something really weird?"

Krystyna laughed, and he was thrilled anew. "Sure."

In the Family

Hi, come in, come in…it's so good to finally meet you! Christy has told me so much about you. She just texted me—she got stuck in traffic on the 101, but she'll be here as soon as she can. And then we can all head out to dinner. Would you like something to drink? Looks like my sister bought some apple cider…and there's a pitcher of sangria if that's more your speed. Sorry, looks like she's out of bottled water, but there's tap? It's an older house, and sometimes the pipes are a little funky.

All right, apple cider it is!

I can tell you some of the family stories about Christy, if you like. She thought she'd never find you, but thank God we have all these great genetics databases now, right? It's so much easier to reconnect with lost family. We can make up for all that lost time!

No, I had no idea you existed, not until Christy told me a few months ago. You'd think she'd have let her own twin sister know about her pregnancy, wouldn't you? But that was a rough time for her, and we hadn't been close for a few years. We were close when we were little kids, but *Ferndale Family Files* drove a bit of a wedge, I'm afraid.

Oh, you hadn't heard that story? My sister started acting before I did. She loved television, and when she saw a casting call for 8-year-old girls for a new sitcom, she begged my mom to let her go. And so she prepared a monologue—I helped her practice it—and even practiced her singing and dancing, just in case. Her excitement about the whole thing was pretty contagious. But she came down with a stomach bug the day before the auditions, and there was no way she could go. And just on impulse, I asked our mom if I could go to the tryout instead. I knew her monologue just about as well as she did, and why not?

I killed it; they cast me as Sally Ferndale, and the rest is history! But unfortunately, Christy…didn't deal with the situation very well. To say that she was upset that I got to star in a sitcom and she didn't…that's a huge understatement.

She was inconsolably angry for a long time. Outraged, really. It was just the worst injustice in her mind.

We all figured she'd get over it, and she did seem to calm down after a bit, but our relationship was never the same. She harbored a grudge for a very long time, even if she wouldn't admit to it. *Couldn't* admit to it. Our mother didn't approve of grudges, especially not for girls. Sugar and spice and all that, right?

Sometimes I think everything would have been better if they'd just put the two of us in a boxing ring and let Christy really give it to me. Just get all that resentment and bitterness out of her system, you know? Men seem to be able to do that kind of thing—be violent and move on.

No, I didn't know about what Larry Flaxman was doing when I was on the show. I did know my costar Jennifer Cairns—she played the middle sister—started acting strangely midway through the first season. And, in hindsight, he was clearly paying inappropriate attention to her. I guess the adults who saw it happening were quick to pretend it was all innocent because he seemed like such a great guy. It seemed like we were all one big happy family, onscreen and off.

And, after all, he was the star. He was the one punching everybody's meal ticket. But I believe her story, and the other girls' stories. 100%, no question.

Me? No, I was too young for him. People call him a pedophile, but that's not exactly the right term. Hebephile? Yes, that sounds right. He went after girls who were 13 or 14…the show didn't run long enough for me to enter his window of attraction.

Looking back, I have no doubt he was a predator, precisely *because* he seemed like such a great guy. That's how they operate: they accumulate social capital and plausible deniability. They build sympathy. If you're Prince Charming to 95% of the people 95% of the time, nobody believes that 5% when you drop the mask and show who you really are. It takes a great actor to pull that off. Think about it—he had to pretend to be two completely different people for *years*, 24/7. As awful as he is, I can admire his artistry. He taught me so much about the craft of performing and how to survive in this wolf-eat-dog business.

But that's not part of your mother's story, is it? Well, our mom saw how upset she was and encouraged me to keep an eye out for gigs for her. But she got her own agent and landed a modeling deal—which ironically was the thing

I'd wanted to do when we were little. So I don't know if her becoming a model was just the universe having a sense of humor or if she deliberately took that opportunity over others out of spite.

Modeling was fine until she reached her mid-teens. Larry wasn't the only predator around, not by a long shot. She was like this perfect, luscious canapé to half the people she met. They just wanted to eat her up. And she loved all that attention. There were parties, and drugs…she ended up in a relationship with a guy in his twenties. Brock Thurman. Mom and Dad did not approve, not at all, and they tried to get her clear of that, but Brock was incredibly charismatic and had Christy snowed. And we heard a rumor he was part of some cult somewhere. Anyhow, Christy turned 16 and sued for emancipation, and got it, and she disappeared off the map for three years. That's when she had you, and then gave you up for adoption.

Yes, we figure that Brock was your biological father, but it's hard to be sure. We never knew a lot about him. I only met him one time. He was good-looking, for sure. Gorgeous brown eyes and thick lashes, like yours. His father was a record exec, I think? He had plenty of money, but no steady job that we could see. Had some bit parts in shows and did a little modeling himself—I'm pretty sure that's how they met. I heard a rumor his father cut off his money and so they got sucked into doing porno movies, but I don't know about that. Frankly, I don't want to know.

Anyhow, she showed back up when she was 19, completely penitent about having left, but she didn't want to talk about where she'd been the previous three years. Mom helped her get her GED and enroll at Los Angeles City College. For a while, it seemed like it would be a fresh start all the way around. I thought she and I could go back to being sisters like we had been before the show wrecked our relationship.

But she still held a grudge. I guess, somewhere along the line, she got it in her head that I deliberately made her sick so she couldn't audition. She thought I had gotten her to eat a sandwich with spoiled lunchmeat on it. Someone— Brock, maybe, but who knows?—had convinced her that I was this pre-teen Machiavellian mastermind ruining her dreams of TV stardom. Silly, right? I can't plan anything more complicated than dinner.

Oh, I wouldn't say that—"crazy" is a really strong word. I think she had been through an emotional meat grinder, and she'd been around a lot of drugs and people who preyed on all her insecurities to keep her under their control. I think they made me into the source of all her troubles to keep her from thinking about what they were doing to her, you know?

Hollywood is full of people who aren't crazy…but they have crazy ideas. For instance, Mrs. Capaldi, who was our studio teacher when I was working on the show. Now, she was a great, great lady, and she loved all of us like we were her own kids. But she'd read all these articles about how dairy products are bad, which they definitely are if you're allergic to them like I am now. At the time, I was not, but she was all, "No milk for you!" She had us drink soy milk instead when we were on set. Soy milk every day. I'm sure I drank a gallon of it every week. And that was fine, for a while, but then I started getting headaches, and one day I broke out in in these godawful itchy hives.

Mom took me to the doctor, and the doctor said I'd developed an allergy to soy. He warned it could get a whole lot worse and become this life-threatening thing. So I obviously quit drinking soy milk and carefully avoided anything with soy in it.

Christy knew all about my allergy. And she was still convinced I'd made her sick, and she still wanted to get back at me.

Now, let me pause for a sec. Christy and I had a long conversation about all of this, and she and I are cool now. Cool about everything. She's made it all up to me. So I'm not telling you this to make you think poorly of your mother. But you're part of the family now, and these are family stories I think you should know, okay?

Okay, good, I'm glad you understand.

So, there was a 4th of July barbecue, hosted by a guy named Greg who we both liked and wanted to go out with. Christy brought a seven-bean salad…and she made it with edamame, and didn't tell me. I'm pretty sure she just wanted me to break out in hives so I'd have to go home and she'd get Greg all to herself.

After three bites of the salad, I felt my throat closing up. Massive anaphylactic shock. Lucky I didn't die. Spent three days in the hospital, and when I got out, I discovered that I'd developed cross-reaction allergies to everything else in the salad, too: black beans, kidney beans, garbanzos, pinto beans, navy beans, wax beans, green beans. There was some cracked wheat and parmesan cheese in there, too, so guess what? I suddenly had wheat and dairy allergies to deal with.

Yeah, my allergies got really bad. My immune system had just gone completely berserk, all because of that stupid salad. One of the immunologists at UCLA ended up publishing a paper about my case; yay for him, I guess? I landed in the ER a couple more times before I figured out I could really only eat leafy vegetables, fruit, fish and meat. Any grains or legumes at all could make me sick. Even quinoa. I knew I could never pull off being a vegan, but I'd wanted to be a vegetarian because I think animals are pretty cool, you know? But that wasn't going to happen.

I got used to the new normal, and things were more or less okay for the next decade. Christy and I had our ups and downs. She was kind of a pain in my ass about my diet—she seemed to think my allergies were all in my head, or that I just wasn't trying hard enough to get over them. Like, how can you just get over an allergy? I took my medicine and avoided problem foods, but she kept trying to get me to eat things she knew I couldn't have. It got old in a hurry, but like I said, we've talked about it and we're cool now.

But a couple of years before I finally got her to understand the gravity of my situation, we were both in North Carolina for gigs and she invited me to go on a hike in the woods. And she didn't warn me about the ticks. I know, I know, that's a common-sense thing, right? Woods equals ticks. But I'm not very outdoorsy, so I just didn't think about what might happen. I got bit by a couple of lone star ticks, and at first I didn't think it was any big deal.

But I had a burger on a lettuce wrap that night, and three hours later I was vomiting and sick and landed in the hospital again. It took the doctors a while to figure out what had happened, but the tick bites gave me an alpha-gal meat allergy. I couldn't eat beef or pork or lamb or goat anymore. Bye bye, bacon.

So I was down to fish and poultry for my protein sources. But I started throwing them up, too, even though all the tests said they should be fine. I started raising my own chickens so I could control what they ate; it didn't help. I lost forty-three pounds, and developed all these other allergies and chemical sensitivities. It was horrible; I couldn't sleep at night from the itching. And I sure as hell couldn't work: I had this terrible, cracking, weeping eczema all over my body. I was not at all ready for my close-up, you know? My agent was just horrified at the condition I was in. So I moved way up into the mountains for the winter, away from the air pollution and pollen, and that helped so, so much. And I got a line on a manufacturer who makes clean protein powder for people like me.

Within a few months of moving and changing my diet, I was doing a whole lot better. The eczema mostly went away, and I'd gained enough weight that I looked pretty again and not like a walking skeleton with skin and hair. My agent agreed I was in fit shape to start looking for new work, even if it was just voice acting.

But Christy was convinced—convinced!—all my allergies were psychosomatic, and that I was turning myself into this crazy antisocial hermit. Ruining my career, she said. She didn't have a boyfriend or a job or anything then, and I think she was a little obsessed with me. Our parents had kind of written her off as a flake and she just didn't have anyone else. And I admit that I was still not over her dragging me into the woods and getting me bitten by ticks. I did not want to see her. At all. But she kept calling me, and emailing me, saying she wanted to talk. And she wore me down, like she always does, and I invited her up to the house.

She strolled in reeking of Chanel. It was like she'd showered in it or something. It instantly gave me this blinding headache. And I'd *told* her at least fifteen times, *do not* wear perfumes to my house. Do. Not.

I blew up at her, and started screaming at her about how disrespectful and inconsiderate she was, and she started screaming back at me about the damned sandwich I don't remember giving her when we were 8.

"I wish you'd starved to death, you ugly cunt!" she yelled at me, and shoved me into my bookcase.

My hand landed on the Emmy Award I won for playing Sally Ferndale, and I just…disconnected for a second.

When I came back to myself, I was standing there with my Emmy in my fist and Christy was lying there in a heap, staring up at nothing. I'd caved her temple in with the base. I don't know if you've ever held an Emmy, but they're pretty heavy. Built to last.

And of course, I had that gut-churning, *oh-shit* moment when I realized I'd done something permanent and stupid.

My head was killing me, though, so I dragged her into the zero-entry shower in the first-floor guest room to wash all the perfume off her. It seemed like the thing to do while I was trying to figure out what the hell I was going to say to the police. As I was rinsing her body, I thought, why does this have to be a bad thing? Maybe this was *meant* to happen.

It hit me like lightning: I could pretend to be her. Nobody would have to know she was dead until I was ready. I had her keys, her wallet, her clothes. Full access to everything in her life. The only people who *might* be able to tell the difference were our parents, and even if they figured it out, I knew they'd never narc on me.

I mean, you couldn't tell, could you?

And because you're family, I know you can keep all this a secret, right?

So there I was in the bathroom, thinking about my sister as an ongoing role, when I had another thought: why let *any* of this go to waste?

I went to the kitchen, and sure enough, I had a couple of cookbooks that had instructions for dressing deer and boar, and others that covered basic butchery. So I got some good sturdy knives and plastic bags and whatnot and went back to the bathroom and took care of her.

She and I had a really good talk while I worked. I think I mentioned that earlier? Yes, it was a little one-sided, but I think she understood me. And I forgave her for everything she'd done to harm me.

And, oh, she's made some great recipes. Anything pork-related has been just *mwah!* Roasts. Steaks. Chops. Stir-fry. I used almost all of her, and the bits I couldn't I cremated in the barbecue out back. Roasted her bones and used them in stock. When I'm done with her, there won't be anything for the CSI folks to find, if they ever get wise.

Oh, no, honey, don't try to get up, you'll just fall—

—whoops, that looked like it hurt. I should put some bumpers on that coffee table. I'm so sorry. Let me get you back onto the sofa, okay? There we go. Looks like the drugs are really getting the better of you now, aren't they?

Why? Is that what you just asked? Well, you were looking so hard for your mom, I figured you'd want to know the whole story.

Oh, you mean, why am I doing *this*? Because I'm nearly out of Christy. And she is so, so good. I just can't go back to nothing but tubs of protein powder and salad; I can't. So I put my DNA out on the databases—which is, conveniently, also *her* DNA—to see who might be a good match. Someone lonely, someone who wouldn't be missed.

I found you. And I'm sorry you won't be missed. It's rough that things went so sideways with your adoptive parents. And it's hard out there for girls who chase boys away with their big scary emotions. You took after Christy a whole lot.

The good news is, it won't hurt. Cross my heart. I promise. You seem like a good kid despite it all; you really do. Your mother would have been so proud of you.

The Kind Detective

One late September Sunday at exactly 4 p.m., Detective Craig McGill was nursing an Irish coffee and poring over the cold-case murder photos spread across his cigarette-pocked kitchen table. His eyes ached. There *had* to be some small but crucial details he missed the first twenty times he studied these black-and-white snapshots of death and misery. He was certain, sure as a priest about the truth of a loving God, that if he just looked at things the right way, he'd solve these grisly puzzles. Justice would be served. And if a horror could be met with no meaningful justice, at least grieving families could finally gain some closure.

A loud *bang!* made him reflexively dive to the worn yellow linoleum floor. His ears popped as if he were on a jet that had taken a sudden 20,000-foot plunge. Vertigo surged bile into his throat as he rolled sideways to draw the .38 revolver he kept in a holster bolted beneath the table.

He crouched in the shadow of the table, waiting for another *bang!* None came. It hadn't been gunfire. Too loud, too low. But it had come from the street in front of his house. Maybe closer. A bomb? His mind flashed on the pressure cooker IEDs the narc squad had recovered from a backwoods meth lab. Who would have tossed a bomb into his yard? The local Klan, angry that he'd sent one of their boys to Angola for murder? Gangbangers? A random lunatic?

After a ten count, he crouch-ran to the living room window and peeked through mini-blinds. The only thing that registered at first was that something was *terribly wrong* with his yard. But for a couple of seconds his brain rejected the missives from his eyes because what he beheld was an impossibility.

The massive pecan tree that shaded the front yard of the shotgun bungalow since his grandfather had built it in 1930 was gone. Not exploded, not burned down—*gone*. It had a canopy as wide as the house and a trunk he couldn't get his arms around and there wasn't a stick or leaf left of it. Not even the main roots remained. A wide, perfectly hemispherical scoop of dirt and concrete sidewalk was gone, too. McGill was relieved that the water and gas mains hadn't been broken.

Nobody was visible on his street except for his catty-corner neighbor, Mrs. Fontenot. He gave her all his pecans every fall, and the pies she made from them were one of the purest joys in his life. Before he tasted one, he'd scoffed at people who declared that this or that food was a religious experience. Mrs. Fontenot made him a believer. Upon taking his first bite, he declared that she should be a pastry chef. She laughed and replied that it would be the ruination of a fine hobby.

Mrs. Fontenot was dressed in her gardening hat and matching lavender gloves and rubber boots and sat beside a scooped crater in her front yard. Her magnolia was gone. She was hunched over, listing to the side in the way that people do when they are in profound shock.

McGill shoved his pistol in the back waistband of his cargo pants and hurried out to see if she needed help. The heavy smells of tree root sap and fresh overturned soil were thick in the humid air. He glanced down at his missing tree's crater as he hurried past it. The remaining roots were cleanly severed at the margin of the hemisphere. What kind of machine could have done such a thing? And why?

"Miz Fontenot, are you okay?" he called as he scanned the street for strange vehicles. His snap judgement that this was the work of criminals he'd crossed seemed ridiculous, now. Someone who could take a pair of big old trees like this could have taken his whole house with him inside it. But someone did do this strange, powerful thing, so maybe the perpetrator was watching? The hand of God hadn't just scooped out their trees. The universe didn't work that way. Did it?

Mrs. Fontenot made no reply to his call, did not move, so he ran over and knelt beside her.

"Miz Fontenot?" He gently touched her shoulder. "Are you okay?"

She slowly turned to face him. Her dark face was wet with tears, and her brown eyes stared wide. He'd once seen that same expression on a small boy who'd watched his father cut up his mother with a hatchet.

"Oh…Detective. So fine of you to visit." Her voice was as flat as a salt marsh.

"Did you see what happened?"

"I saw…I saw…"

She started to weep. Deep, wracking, soul-wrenching sobs. People her age who got this upset sometimes had heart attacks or strokes. McGill wondered if he should call for a squad, but he wasn't sure if she had health insurance. If she didn't, the ambulance and ER bills might break her. She didn't seem to be in immediate danger. Maybe she just needed a chance to rest and gather herself?

"Can you stand up? Let's get you inside. I'll make you some tea."

He gently helped her up and escorted her back into her house. She stopped crying, but her whole body shook as if she were walking through snow. Shock, definitely. He got her settled in her easy chair, pulled off her boots, and tucked a crocheted green afghan over her legs so she'd stay warm.

"Thank you, detective. You're a kind man. Don't let nothing tell you otherwise."

McGill smiled at her, feeling relieved that she was able to speak, and went into her kitchen to put the kettle on.

When he returned with a steaming mug of chamomile tea, Mrs. Fontenot was dead.

The purely practical part of McGill's mind told him that the EMTs wouldn't have arrived in time to save her. They just wouldn't bust the speed limit for a black lady with vague symptoms, not even if a white off-duty cop was calling on her behalf. And *that* renewed realization—the system he served was horribly flawed—made the mess of sadness, anger and guilt stewing in his skull almost boil over.

He hadn't shed a single tear at any of the terrible murder scenes he'd investigated. Nobody wanted an emotional cop. It was not *professional*, it was not *manly*, and he would not weep now for this sweet old lady slumped in her favorite chair, even if nobody could possibly see him.

He would not cry. He would do his job: find out who did this to her. This wasn't *technically* murder, but he was sure to his core that whoever took her tree, took her life just the same. He would work this like any other case, and he would solve it, and there would be justice.

When McGill arrived at the police station early the next morning, he found his partner Rhett Gradney arguing with Cindy Romero, one of their narcotics detectives.

"This whole tree thing is stupid, and we shouldn't waste resources on it." Gradney looked royally pissed off, which meant he was probably scared. Yep, he was bouncing his left foot. In the five years they'd worked cases together, McGill had learned all Gradney's tells.

"How can you say that?" Romero's eyes were hard coals; her stance told him she was ready to sock him in the jaw. "A dozen people ended up in the hospital yesterday, scared into heart attacks or nervous breakdowns."

"At least one landed in the morgue." McGill felt just as irritated as Romero looked. He stepped past them to fetch his coffee cup from his desk. "My neighbor saw her tree get taken, and she died not five minutes later."

Gradney's face flushed firetruck red. "Goddammit, not you, too. Of all the people here my own damn partner should see how idiotic this whole thing is!"

"Mrs. Fontenot was a great lady, and she's gone." McGill looked his partner square in the eyes. He didn't want to antagonize him, but he hated it when Gradney tried to pretend that unpleasant things just weren't happening. Denial was not a useful or admirable trait in a detective. "Maybe whoever took her tree and put a big ol' hole on her land didn't mean for her to die, but she's dead. And if they *did* mean to do it, that's aggravated criminal damage to property."

"It's a fucking tree!" Gradney was screaming now, and everyone else in the station had turned to stare. "Trees are everywhere! Why get so scared over losing a damn tree that you have a heart attack? Just fucking plant a new one and move on! And why steal trees? That's some goddamned cheesy 60s Batman villain shit! None of this makes a lick of sense!"

"Detective Gradney." Police Chief Sammons glared at him from his office doorway. "You seem stressed, son. You need to take the day off?"

"No, sir." Gradney's blush deepened, spread. His scalp looked like a tomato under his short blond buzzcut.

"Then use your goddamn inside voice." Sammons looked like he was trying to set him on fire with his mind.

Gradney averted his gaze. "Yes, sir."

"Chief." Romero crisply stepped forward and stood at parade rest. "Is there a plan for how to pursue this tree situation?"

Seeming mildly annoyed at her question, Sammons glanced from her to McGill to Gradney.

"There is no specific plan at present." His reply was calm and slow. "A few minutes ago, I spoke with the mayor, and he's inclined to treat this as a serial vandalism incident. The newspapers are framing this as the work of Halloween pranksters. We're going along with that for now, until we figure out what in the name of little green men is really happening here. No sense in making people panic."

McGill wanted to tell them all that it wasn't just the trees; Mrs. Fontenot had seen something terrible that broke her heart. He was willing to bet solid money that everyone in the hospital had seen it, too. But saying that out loud might make him look like a lunatic.

So instead, he nodded at Sammons and said, "Panic kills, sir. Nobody here wants that."

He realized Romero was giving him a hard sideways stare, and when he met her gaze, she shrugged as if to say, *Sorry, buddy, I tried, but you're on your own.*

As the day went on, the police station buzzed with scorn and disbelief over the trees. McGill decided to keep his investigation to himself, but every disparaging remark reinforced his resolve to pursue it. He started taking late lunch breaks to patrol neighborhoods with big old oaks, elms, walnuts, pecans, birches, magnolias and ashes.

By Thursday, he'd identified a definite pattern. Each day at 4 p.m., someone or something would scoop up a half-dozen trees from various nearby locations. And then five minutes after that, the town due west would get hit. And then a little while later, the next town over. The phenomenon was global, it seemed, and followed perhaps not the sun, but certainly the turn of the Earth.

People were dying. Property was destroyed. The whole town was pocked with craters. This was clear. And yet, authority figures and talking heads still weren't taking it very seriously. News reports and official announcements remained sparse and dismissive; even the tabloid shows that usually exploited any possible reason to scare their audiences were avoiding the subject. McGill still felt echoes of his own disorientation and his mind's initial refusal to see his own tree's abduction. He knew why reporters and cops and mayors were doing all that hand-waving. They had to pretend that this incomprehensible display of power wasn't any big deal, or the fabric of order holding the town together might fall apart.

People needed to know that their lives were governed by predictable forces. The law mattered because it mapped order and safety onto the chaos of human interactions. Justice wasn't just a matter of punishing the guilty; citizens needed to see that people would genuinely get what they deserved. People who worked hard and behaved decently would get to have beach vacations and nice houses with comfortable porches shaded by big pecan trees and friendly neighbors who made sublime pies. Those who didn't had to change their ways. And if they wouldn't change, well, they had to be removed so they couldn't hurt decent folk. McGill never felt good when he heard that petty criminals he'd busted got killed in prison, but he refused to feel badly about sending them away. Crimes had to have consequences. They *had* to.

Though the brass wouldn't admit a serious crime was even happening, McGill made sure that at 3:45 every day he was on patrol in neighborhoods with big old trees. He hoped to spot an abduction, or at least find a witness who could provide some solid details. Suffering a nervous breakdown was not a concern of his. The gruesome violence he'd seen and smelled was stuff they'd never put in scary movies. There were things that even eager gorehounds turned away from, and McGill had gazed upon them with clear eyes. *His* mind was sound.

He drove with his windows down so he could better hear a telltale *bang!* And a strange thing happened. A couple of minutes before an incident, the air took on an electric vibration, and he shivered as if someone was dancing on his grave. The weird frissons got stronger the closer he was to an abduction site.

Following those new instincts led him to be on Willowbrook Avenue right as a tree was taken. There was the *bang!* loud as a stun grenade. He turned to see a green blur shooting straight up into the sky from a nearby yard. For the first time, he realized the trees were whisked away so damn fast they broke the sound barrier.

The sheer improbability of it made his mind reel, but he saw a blue-uniformed postman staring down into the fresh crater, his mail bag slumped at his feet, and McGill's instincts took over.

"Sir, did you see what just happened?" he called as he pulled over.

The postman slowly turned toward him, and began to laugh. He was medium height, wiry, and looked like his folks might be Vietnamese. From the anguished expression on his face, McGill figured he was going to burst into tears at any moment.

The detective got out of his car and slowly approached. "Sir, are you all right?"

"I…I wanted to see," the postman gasped between giggles. "I just couldn't not try to see, you know?"

McGill nodded. "I want to see, too. Can you tell me what you saw?"

"Don't do it, man. You don't want to know. He's…he's gonna run out. And then everything is…is…." He started weeping, and looked a gnat's breath away from completely losing it. "Just…go back to your family. Take that trip to Six Flags the kids have been bugging you about."

"I don't have a family. I just have my job." McGill didn't have a good read on whether he was dangerous or not. He did *not* want to be one of those cops who shot down an innocent person because of their own cowardice. He knew the department would back him if the kill was even slightly justified, but he didn't think he could look himself in the mirror ever again if he ended someone who'd needed his help. "I need to find out what's going on. Can you help me understand this?"

The postman shook his head. Tears and snot flowed down his face. "Go to Vegas, then. Anything but this. *Anything.*"

McGill reflexively stepped back and dropped his hand to his belt holster as the man reached into his pocket and pulled out a box cutter. "Easy, there."

"Sorry. I can't help anyone." The postman clicked the blade open and plunged it into his own neck. His punctured carotid artery spurted an impressive gout of blood that splattered on McGill's shoes. A second later, he fell to his knees on the grass.

The detective was about to step forward to try to put some compression on the wound when his entire body rashed in goosebumps and all the hairs rose on his neck and arms. The frisson was more powerful than ever. A tree nearby was about to go. He scanned the street and saw an oak that had to be a hundred years old in the front yard of a pink house. *Yes.*

McGill turned away from the dying postman and sprinted across the street toward the oak. The trunk was as thick as a car and the limbs creaked low under their own weight. Its hard leaves rattled in the breeze. This was the 30-pound trophy bass of trees. He felt a consuming excitement he hadn't experienced since the night they'd closed in on the Savetier Killer who'd been murdering cops and security guards across the state.

He felt *alive* in a way that he hadn't in years.

Just as he got within a few feet of the spreading canopy, it happened. His ears popped from the pressure change as something like a huge invisible punch rammed down from the sky, and then the *bang!* made him feel as if a 300-pound linebacker had body-slammed him. But he kept his feet, and as he saw the green blur he leaped forward, looking skyward.

And he saw into the hole in the sky.

The vertigo he'd felt before was nothing compared to what he felt now as his mind and vision were dragged in the wake of the tree, hurtling billions of miles into the far reaches of outer space, a distance so vast and cold that no one could ever reach it using human technology.

And in that moment, he witnessed a scene with perfect clarity. A swollen red sun larger than most star systems cast a sullen crimson glare across its galaxy. And silhouetted against that sun was an old god, curled like a deformed, tumorous fetus the size of Jupiter. The thing was more grotesque than a million bloody crime scenes. It was more twisted than the worst dreams of the most debased psychopath. McGill couldn't bring himself to behold it entirely; he could at best focus on a patch of scabrous scales here, a planet-sized claw there. He was sure that if he tried to see it wholly his brain would melt.

The abhorrent god slept in death in the harsh radiation, and yet it was not truly dead, and could never die. Orbiting around the cosmic monstrosity were hundreds of thousands of trees. Some were already desiccated, scorched husks, but some keened silently as they both burned and froze in that terrible airless space.

It opened one vast, star-pupiled eye and gazed back at McGill. And the detective knew its abyssal mind. The god, in its own way, was lonely. It wanted to surround itself with dying things to comfort itself. Trees took a while to die. But the god was older than the star it orbited, and its need was endless. It would run out of trees. And then it would drag every man, woman, and child up into that faraway red desolation to die in terror and torment in its vile, alien orbit.

McGill fell backward onto the lawn as the vision released him. He lay there stunned, weeping, his certainties and beliefs a blasted desolation. This was the first time he'd cried in 25 years, and he didn't care. There was no God but the one he'd witnessed, and it cared nothing for human justice or order or anything else he held dear. The only thing that was real was the certainty of death.

And the detective could not imagine anything more horrible than being dragged away from Mother Earth to feed that cosmic abomination. It wasn't just the agony of feeling your flesh boil off your bones and your eyeballs rupture in your skull. It wasn't just the horror of having that monster be the last thing you saw before you died. It was witnessing everything you loved and believed in and had strived for destroyed and mocked by the Universe as you were snuffed out. Billions of people would break and die in that terrible place and there would be no point or greater good or Heaven at the end of it all.

In that moment, the detective wanted to end himself as the postman had. It would be so easy to draw his revolver, blast his own brains across the grass, and be done with it. He'd die in the warm embrace of Earth. And that was the best anyone could hope for now.

"No," McGill whispered to himself. *I have a job. People need me.*

"Oh, my goodness." An elderly white woman with an aluminum cane had emerged from the pink house. She was dressed in a flowered shift and a white shawl. Her slippers were a dingy grey. "Are you okay, sir?"

"Yes, ma'am." He climbed to his feet. "Thank you for asking."

She adjusted her spectacles. "What…what happened to my tree?"

"Nothing happened to your tree, ma'am. Everything is fine."

He drew his revolver and shot her right between the eyes.

"I'm sorry, ma'am," he told her bleeding corpse. "But this is the kindest thing I can think to do."

He went back to his idling car and headed toward the nearest gun shop. He'd need a whole lot more ammunition for his new work. Someone would stop him, sooner or later. Maybe his partner Gradney would shoot him down. That wouldn't be so bad. It was a funeral suit that fit.

In the meantime, though, he needed to be as kind as he could possibly be.

A Preference For Silence

Veronica was a spaceworthy lass with a definite preference for silence and a great sensitivity to detail. She'd never lost her tea in zero gee and had always been the first to note when the coffee maker needed cleaning or when the fluorescent lights would flick-flicker in signal of the bulbs' impending death. Furthermore, she seemed to genuinely relish freeze-dried food.

When the other colonists asked her to take the long watch over *The Doubtful Guest* as it hurtled through space to their new home, she was quietly enthused and declared she'd always meant to read the world's Great Literature.

But they worried that she would get lonely with nothing but books and the hum of the cryopods to keep her company over those dark decades. And, more important, who would watch the ship's systems while she slept?

So they chose a lad named Melvin to be her companion. He matched Veronica in most important aspects: religious affiliation, political outlook, favorite dessert, air freshener preference. While not as attuned to detail as she, he did seem like a fairly alert fellow, respected quiet, and was easily amused by a variety of odd hobbies.

The voyage started well, with Veronica reading the Bronte sisters and Melvin building tiny Spanish galleons out of toothpicks, glue and dental floss. They traded shifts, she awake while he slept, and so they seldom saw one another. When they did, they attempted sex a few times, quietly groping each other beside his mother's cryopod, but it never seemed as satisfying as their respective pastimes.

The trouble began two years into the trip, when Veronica had started on the Russians and Melvin had begun knitting long, itchy black-and-blond scarves from all the hair they'd shed. It was not the aesthetic qualities of the scarves that upset her, for she approved of creative approaches to waste management. Nor did the click-clack of his needles bother her as she slept. It was his snoring.

His snore developed slowly, like cancer. When she began *The Brothers Karamazov*, it was just a soft, throaty purr like the breathing of an asthmatic cat. Barely noticeable. A few months later, when she was on *Notes From the Underground*, the purr became punctuated with the occasional grunt or snort, and by the time she finished the ship's store of Dostoyevsky and started *Anna Karenina*, his snore had risen in volume to resemble the revving of a small motorcycle with a bad cylinder.

Veronica, who read slowly because she liked to savor every word, could not concentrate with all that infernal noise. She wrestled with issues of politeness and protocol for a few days, then woke Melvin and suggested they re-synchronize their schedules so that they were awake at the same time. He reluctantly agreed after she promised to program an extra set of monitors to sound an alarm if anything should happen while they slept.

With the snoring gone, Veronica happily resumed her normal reading rate of ten pages a day. But then she started to notice other things about Melvin that disturbed her. The click-clack of his knitting needles made it hard for her to focus on all the nuances of Tolstoy's use of the verb "to be", and the sound of him gargling in the morning broke her concentration entirely.

She did not approach him with her complaints because she felt a bit sheepish for making him adjust his sleeping schedule to salve her sensibilities. After all, he'd taken her imposition with such good spirit. And, as her dear departed mother had always taught her, it simply wasn't polite to comment on others' personal habits.

So she tried to concentrate on her text. But more malignant Melvinisms arose. The crunching of him eating his daily ration of vegetable flakes. The wet slurping sound he made when he drank his coffee. The way the air whistled through his nose when he sighed. The low, animal grunts he made when he whipped himself with one of his scarves behind his mother's cryopod.

Finally, one morning a few days before Halloween back on Earth, Melvin was drinking his coffee and knitting in the nude. And then he belched. Not a mild little burp, but an eructation that shook the whole ship, thundering like the Four Horsemen of the Apocalypse.

Her patience snapped along with her concentration. She threw down *War and Peace*, launched herself across the room and started to strangle Melvin with his scarf. He made quite a lot of noise, but only for a little while. When he was unconscious, she stabbed him fifty-three times with the knitting needles, then hauled him and his scarves, toothpick ships, fungus sculptures and rotifer farm to the airlock and ejected everything into the cold silence of outer space.

Feeling exquisitely relieved, she washed her hands, carefully dried them and resumed her reading.

But then she started to notice the low hum of the cryopods, the periodic hiss of the cooling units. The flutter of the air vents. The raggedness of her own breathing. The lub-dup of her own heart.

Her hands began to shake.

Wake Up Naked Monkey You're Going to Die

The ketamine-laced tranquilizer dart was wearing off. Jimbo raised his head, but all he could see were the glowing rainbow sprites swirling above him, moth-fluttering around the smoky oaky torches bolted to the cavern's ceiling. Pretty lights, oo, he'd love to float among them like a supernaut. If only he wasn't tied down to this rusty old mistletoe throne.

"Santa's comin' to town!" yelled the Feeb. "Jigglin' like a bowl fulla jelly!"

His shouts cut Jimbo's brain-haze like a razorblade on a punch-swollen eyelid. Thank God for ol' Feeb; he missed the Brainy Train all right, but what wits he was dealt never went dull, no matter how much eggnog or weed was in his system.

The Alleygat Autocrats had surely spat gigantic rainbows in all their minds, but Feeb, he knew how to keep everyone on course. A coarse, hoarse course, of course. Fuck him and the horse he coursed in on…

Jimbo's head fell sleepy-dead to his spattered chest.

"Jingle all the way, motherfuckers!" screeched the Feeb.

"Wakey bakey," Jimbo snorted, his eyes popping open. He focused in on Bobby, who lay in a darkening pool of stickiness. The monster's elves had bobbed his legs clean off below the knee. A gummy machete lay mere feet away, just out of reach.

Fucking elves, Jimbo thought, his head clearing a bit more. What kind of nihilistic fuckclowns firebombed their own city and worshipped a big jiggly sonic death Santa that wanted to apocalyze the whole planet? Taint Nicholas could've promised to shit pure gold in their stockings for all Jimbo knew, but who could cash it in if the world was cashed out? Stupid mooks.

Jimbo saw Bobby's chest rise and fall. His leg vessels had probably rolled up inside the stumps, saving him from a quick bleeding death so he could look forward to slowly melting in the belly of the beast.

Ain't life a sugarplum? Always cut down and not across, kids, Jimbo thought.

"Hey Bobby," Jimbo called, his throat as dry and scratchy as the red and green gift ribbons binding his wrists behind the wrought-iron throne. "Wake up, Bobby."

They'd crippled Bobby because he was the strong one, the one they couldn't rely on drugs and twisty satin holding. Now Jimbo had to be Hercules. But first he had to bust free of this damned chair.

He craned his neck at the Feeb, who'd been strung up on meathooks through the flesh of his back in a suicide suspension amongst the huge glass Christmas ornaments decorating the ceiling. Most of the balls contained the melting corpses of shopping mall Santas. Poor bastards never stood a chance. The Feeb would survive, if they got him down and to a doctor before infection set in.

They were in a freaking charnel house; the greasy remains of countless more Santas and Salvation Army bell-ringers lay in festering puddles around them. The worst, most bitter of him thought it served them all right for getting their jingle on in October. They ought to at least let Thanksgiving dinner settle before they busted out the Saint Nick schtick. There were real monsters about at Halloween.

Hunt the Wumpus. Raise a rumpus, he wants to jump us…crap, stay focused! he thought.

"Bobby! BOBBY!"

Bobby stirred and faintly laughed.

Jimbo knew Bobby was off bouncing in Happyfunball Land like he'd been. Still was. He had to give them both something to focus on.

"Bobby, did you know that Catholic priests can bless beer?" he asked. "They can even bless seismograph machines."

"You're shitting me," mumbled Bobby.

"No, I am being completely true with you. A Catholic priest could most especially bless that machete beside you, even though it's done you wrong, like that gal in that country song. You got no legs, Bobby, so don't try to walk, but get that blade and crawl over here with it. Bobby!"

"I got no legs?" Bobby started to drunkenly hum a Monty Python tune.

"Think of the nice blessed seismograph! 'St. Emidius, pray for us, and in the name of Jesus Christ of Nazareth, protect us and also this seismograph from the terror of earthquakes,' the nice priest says. Save us from the terror of Apocalypse Santa, Bobby Boy. You've *got* to."

"I can be abundingly Van Helsingly heroic now, Jimbo," Bobby replied, reaching for the machete. He gripped it, and started to king-snake forward, then went slack, his eyes glazed. "Pretty pretty blood, is it all mine?"

The Feeb wailed and fought his fleshhook chains. "Ring ring ring the devil's calling! He stuck his jingle balls in our Halloween pie! Come out, come out wherever you are!"

"Beer is life, Bobby! Bring the machete," Jimbo implored. "It's Miller time for sure! We gotta hump or we're skunked!"

A low, weirdly modulated rumble rolled from a nearby tunnel. "HO HO HO…"

It was the sound of a thousand pounds of ancient clotted slime dragging itself across the floor of the catacombs.

"HO HO HO HO…"

Each booming *HO* was the sound of pure impending death, a sound older than evolution, a cosmic alarm clock blaring *WAKE UP NAKED MONKEY YOU'RE GOING TO DIE!* Every rat brain would fear it like the roar of an exploding star.

Jimbo saw Bobby's pupils expand as the adrenaline hit his blood, and suddenly Bobby was up on rawtorn hands and knees scrabbling to the back of Jimbo's chair, sawing at the knotted ribbons. Jimbo felt the satin give and he pulled his hands free, swinging his arms in a pitcher's windmill.

A Catholic priest could bless anything. A perfect, crystalline memory surfaced, lit by synaptic fire: the shutout game he'd pitched against St. Francis DeSales in high school. Their coach Father Santoro blessed his baseballs before the game: *May God guide your arm like he guided David's sling against Goliath, and with the Lord's help we're gonna beat the snot out of those smug little trust-fund turds at St. Francis. Amen.*

He felt in his pocket for their salvation: the aluminum jar of caustic salt was still there. The last priest alive in the city had blessed it. The elves didn't think to strip them of anything but obvious weapons. Stupid mooks.

"HO HO HO HO *HOOOOO…*"

The ancient acidic God Slime Santa flopped into the flickering torchlight like an enormous, unholy figgy pudding twinkling with a million emerald eyes and tufted with the whitest beard hairs. The occasional rosy cheek or cherry-like nose rose up from the jiggling mass of ectoplasmic flesh and disappeared again. Some folks whispered that this foul god had other forms in the past, but for decades its green-robed worshippers had fed it mall Santas and bell-ringers, and now it mimicked its prey in a thousand ever-changing perversions of the essence of old Father Christmas. Gazing upon it and trying to assemble its squirming parts into a proper Santa was a purely mind-breaking experience.

Each sonorous *HO* was getting louder, the stone walls shuddering, Jimbo's teeth rattling in his jawbone. They only had a few susurrous heartbeats until it reached the deadly tone to batter bones and muscles to pulp, liquefying their flesh so the acidic abomination could sponge them into its hundred jolly stomachs.

Jimbo pulled out the blessed jar and gripped it splitfingered for a fastball. He whispered, "Sing a song of sixpence, slimeball, 'cause I got a pocket full of lye!" He wished to himself, prayed to God and pitched as hard as he could. The shiny jar hit the mark and sank fast into the beast's hungry red flank.

The God Slime Santa's ravenous jelly ate through the aluminum, and suddenly its innards started blistering, bubbling, foaming. The caustic salts bloomed whitely inside the translucent flesh. The holiday monster thrashed, melting faster than a sugar witch in a rainstorm, hissing a Christmas carol that was pure delight to the heroes and ghosts listening, rejoicing in the vanquished catacombs.

The Great VüDü Teen Linux Zombie Massacree

Bob and I attracted a pack of zombies when we stopped to fuel up at the Texaco in Buffalo Springs. I hoped we'd lost them, but hope was all I had. Bob said they were the fresh remains of a high school football team who'd been drowned and de-souled by water daemons at a lakeside Halloween party.

Young, strong corpses have the speed and stamina to run down a deer. Until the sun and wind finally turned their flesh to stinky jerky, they'd be dangerous enough to make a vampire crap bats. And fresh zombies are persistent as porn site pop-up ads. If they take a shine to the smell of your blood, they might track you for days, stopping only if live meat falls right in their laps

It'd be months before they got the Dead Man Shamble and could be taken out with a well-placed head shot. Of course, with the right software and hardware, you could kill even the most problem zombie, but that was some fairly arcane stuff, even for experienced hackers.

If my editor was right, Bob was one of only about five genuine cyberspiritual experts in the U.S. But so far he seemed more like a second-rate grease monkey than a computer guru. I had my doubts.

"Maybe we should go back to the gas station," I suggested. "That guy Bubba said he had a sick badger in one of his pens. Wouldn't this work better with a fresh animal?"

More important, Bubba had plenty of guns and ammunition; all I had was a small 6-shot Beretta in the thigh pocket of my cargo pants. Bob had a small deer rifle in the gun rack of his cab. Not nearly enough firepower if the zombie teen squad showed up.

"'Taint no challenge, little lady," Bob said, his voice dripping with scorn and tobacco juice. "Any fool with a copy o' Red Hat and a pair of pliers can put Linux on a live badger, or even a fresh-kilt one."

Bob hit a pothole, and I nearly lost my grip on my old iPhone. My nice shiny new Samsung phone had fallen out of my pocket when the dead kid in the tattered Donald Trump costume was chasing me through the parking lot by the gas pumps, and I'd be damned if I was going to lose anything else on this trip.

I was going to kill my editor for sending me on this Texas Hellride. Absolutely kill her. Or at least demand a paid vacation. I could still hear Wendy's simpering wheedle: "The highway patrol says the Lubbock area is all clear; you'll be perfectly safe, Sarah."

Safe, my butt.

Bob was warming to his rant. "This zombie business is war. War, little lady, the kind Patton never dreamt of. We are fighting the gall-darned Forces o' Darkness. We gotta use some serious finesse, and there ain't nothing that spells finesse like installing a home defense system on a dead badger. You write that down, little lady. The readers o' MacHac need to know this stuff if they're gonna keep them an' theirs safe."

I dutifully typed it down on my iPhone. I'd gotten pretty quick with the screen keyboard, but as a precaution against being dropped in the mud I'd stuck it down in a sandwich bag, which added an extra layer of challenge to note-taking.

"Hot damn, come to Papa!" Bob abruptly swerved over onto the shoulder and slammed on the brakes. The Ford slewed to a stop in the caliche beside a stand of mesquites.

In the glow of the headlights was a dead badger, all four legs stiff in the air. It was on the large side, maybe close to twenty pounds. Bob hopped out of the truck and ran over to the badger, turning it over and feeling around in the blood-matted fur.

"The legs and spine and skull are in right fine shape," he yelled back to me, as excited as a ten-year-old on Christmas morning. "I can't feel nothing but some broke ribs. This'll do!"

He tossed the badger into the bed of the truck, and soon we were speeding back to Bob's shop.

Bob's Computer Shack was wedged in between a hair salon and a Subway sandwich shop in a little roadside strip. The big storefront windows on all the shops had been boarded up with plywood sheets and reinforced with two-by-fours and rebar; all the shopkeepers were relying on neon "Open" signs to tell passersby that they were carrying on with business in the face of the zombie apocalypse.

I followed Bob into the shop and he locked and barred the door behind us. The air smelled of dust and plastic with a faint metallic stink from a burned-out monitor he'd hauled in for parts. Soon, it was all going to reek of rotten badger. Bob carried the carcass over to a work table he'd already cleared off and covered with a long sheet of butcher paper. He wiped his hands off on his overalls and pulled out an ancient tangerine iBook, which he set on the other end of the table. I pulled out my phone to take notes.

"Okay, first the easy crap: puttin' the Duppy card in the iBook so's we can get OSX to talk to the badger," Bob said. "I already downloaded a copy of FleshGolem from the Apple site—it's in the Utilities section."

Bob pulled what looked like a wireless notebook card out of a drawer of the table. It had a hinged lid and a clear cover over a small, shallow ivory box inlaid in the card.

"Next, you take some hair and blood from the critter and put them in this here compartment." He popped the cover open and smeared a hairy clot into the box.

Bob lifted the keyboard off the iBook to reveal the Airport slot. He slid the Duppy card inside, replaced the keyboard, and set the iBook aside.

I heard a thump and a shriek from the hair salon next door.

"Marla, git yer shotgun!" I heard a woman holler.

The woman sounded a little like Wendy, though the only time I'd ever really heard my editor scream was when a college intern lost an entire set of page proofs. Mostly she just took on a fakey-sweet patronizing tone when she thought you'd screwed up: "Well, we'll do this better next time, now won't we, Sarah?" She talked down to practically everyone like we were preschoolers. No wonder she'd been divorced twice.

Damn her for sending me out here. If I survived this, I was gonna demand vacation and a shiny new workstation

"Okay, now we gotta install the Duppy security antenna," Bob said, apparently oblivious to the shouting next door. "You can run your badger without it, but it'd be pretty easy for someone to hack him if they could get some blood and hair offa it."

I jumped as the shotgun boomed twice in rapid succession next door. A chorus of zombies roared in pain.

"I *told* them they need a better lock on their back door," Bob grumbled. He got a penknife and made a small incision at the nape of the badger's neck. He picked up a long, thin, coppery wire and shoved it down into the incision like a mechanic forcing a rusty dipstick into a car engine. "You gotta get this to lay as flat on the spine as possible, or your security won't be good."

Now somebody was firing a pistol, the pops punctuating the zombie roars.

"Shouldn't we go see if they need help?" I asked.

"Those gals know how to handle themselves. Opening the door right now's a bad idea."

He wiped his hands off and pulled out a bright yellow software box with a cartoon of a witch doctor on the cover. "Now we get to the fun part. We're gonna install VüDü; it's a wicked little Linux distro. If your badger's got some kinda brain damage, you can do a modified install, but it's a real bitch. And rabies makes the whole thing a crapshoot. Read the frickin' manual before you try it."

My heart bounced as dead fists hammered the plywood protecting the computer shop's front windows. I couldn't hear anything from next door; I hoped that meant the women inside had driven their attackers away.

"Don't pay that no nevermind; even if they got through the wood, they still got to get through the window bars. We got plenty o' time."

Bob pulled a small, rolled-up piece of parchment out of his desk. "This has the system config info, spiritual program components, and your password. You gotta write it all down on blessed parchment in something like Enochian or SoulScript. Write neatlike. Roll it up, and stick it down the badger's throat, all the way into the stomach." He demonstrated with the aid of a screwdriver.

The zombies were still hammering the plywood. A couple of them had found a loose edge and were wrenching one panel away from the bricks. One shoved a gray arm between the bars. The pane fractured and fragments shattered to the floor.

My hands were shaking too hard to take notes, so I set my iPhone aside and dug my Beretta out of my thigh pocket. Not that I was in much condition to shoot straight, either.

"You ain't gonna need that yet," Bob said sharply, apparently irritated I'd stopped taking notes. "Them bars'll keep 'em back better than that little peashooter you got there."

I reluctantly stuck the pistol in my waistband and picked up my phone.

He opened the VüDü box and pulled out an herb-scented scroll of paper. "This is the entire code behind VüDü. Fold it up into the shape of the critter, and put more blood and hair inside."

He unrolled the scroll and started folding it up into an origami badgerlike shape. "It's real hard to make your own paper, so don't lose it. Open-source only takes you so far with this stuff."

The zombies had wrenched the first plywood sheet clean off the window. Three of them were growling and rattling the bars while the others hammered and yanked at the remaining boards. My stomach was twisting itself into an acidic knot; the bars really didn't look that sturdy. With every good pull, I could see the steel bolts in the cinderblocks giving, just a little. I wondered how far I'd get if I made a run for the back door.

I cursed Wendy a thousand ways. A vacation and new computer wouldn't even begin to make up for this trip.

Bob was studiously ignoring the zombies. Finished with the origami badger, he smeared a foot-wide pentagram on the paper using the badger's blood. He set the carcass at the top point, and put the origami badger in the middle.

"Now, burn the paper an' do your incantation." He got out his lighter, opened up the VüDü manual, and started chanting while he lit the paper. Bright green flames erupted, and the smoke curled around the badger's carcass. We watched as the smoke flowed into the badger's mouth and nose. It shuddered as it took a breath.

"We got badger!" He pulled out the tangerine iBook and started typing furiously.

The badger was trying to get up, its rigor-mortised legs jerking like Harryhausen stop-motion. It got its head up and growled at us, baring long canines. It sounded more like an angry grizzly bear; I didn't think something that small could generate such menace. I took a step back, just to be safe.

"An' that's why they call them badgers, little lady…when they get mad, they're real bad news!" He laughed. "Nothin' pisses critters off like bein' woke from a good dirt nap."

I was feeling sicker by the minute. I'd had my doubts about the reanimation working, but it had never occurred to me that he wouldn't have the thing under control. The zombies had pulled the rest of the plywood off the window and were heaving hard on the creaking bars.

Bob opened a Telnet window and started tapping in commands. "Junkyard dogs ain't got nothin' on badgers. I seen a 15-pound badger send a 60-pound pit bull mix yelpin' and bleedin' back to his mama. I mean, lookit the claws on this sucker. This bad boy could dig his way through highway pavement—"

The badger abruptly lurched to its feet and leaped on Bob, chomping down on his left forearm. Bob hollered and fell backwards into a table of disassembled PCs. The badger worried his arm furiously as it tore at his belly with its clawed forelegs.

I started forward to try to help Bob, but he waved me back frantically with his free hand.

"No! Git the iBook! Type in 'kill 665'!"

I did. The badger froze, still latched onto Bob's forearm. His tee shirt was soaked in blood from the deep slashes in his belly. He awkwardly shook his arm, but the badger wouldn't budge.

"Well that's a helluva system bug," he said weakly. "This little bastard's bit me right down to the bone. Launch FleshGolem, would ya? It's in the Dock."

I spotted a dock icon that looked like Frankenstein's Monster and clicked it. A program opened that looked a lot like the Mac port of the old DOOM first-person shooter game. Instead of a game screen there was a pixelated black-and-white image of Bob's face.

I was seeing through the dead badger's eyes.

"Cool," I whispered.

"Yeah, it's real cool, get this critter offa me! Hit the 'escape' key!"

The badger unclenched its jaws and fell to the floor with a heavy thump. The screen told me the badger was resetting itself. Bob clutched his bleeding arm, wincing. The badger righted itself and sat like a dog, awaiting new commands. The blood on Bob's shoes shone like tar through the eyecam screen.

"Dang, this stings," Bob said. "Where'd I put that medical kit, I gotta—"

The bars hit the pavement outside with a tremendous clanging crash. One zombie was pinned beneath the bars, but the other four poured in through the shattered window.

"Aw, dangit! Can't a man finish a presentation 'round here?"

Bob pulled a shotgun from a shelf beneath the work table and fired it at the rushing zombies. My ears rang from the boom. The blast hit the lead zombie squarely in its chest, but it barely slowed down.

"Git back an' get the badger running," Bob called loudly, apparently a bit deafened. "An' don't forget to initialize NecroNull in 'options', or he ain't gonna be much use."

Clutching the iBook, I ran to the back of the shop and spotted a closetlike restroom. I ran inside, flipped on the light, and locked the door behind me. The lock wouldn't hold for more than a minute or two, but I hoped Bob could keep the zombies busy long enough to figure out what I was doing.

Amid the roars and shotgun blasts, I set the iBook on the sink and moused around, trying to get the badger up and biting

While the basic controls were indeed fairly simple and DOOMlike, there was menu after menu of advanced controls for a mindboggling array of behaviors. There was even a Karaoke menu so that you could hook up a microphone and attempt to speak through the primitive vocal cords of the creature you'd reanimated.

Pushing aside the mental image of a frat boy drunkenly singing "Louie Louie" through a dead Pomeranian, I found the NecroNull combat option and clicked it on.

The eyecam screen shuddered and turned technicolor. A new menu of fighting commands popped up for regular Kombat mode and IKnowKungFu mode, the latter of which came with a warning that it was only good for five minutes before your golem spontaneously combusted.

My inner 15-year-old giggled: *Spontaneous combustion? Fire is cool! Fire fire fire!*

I told my teen to buzz off and set to kicking some zombie hiney in Kombat mode.

All I could see was a mass of legs, so I hopped the badger onto a nearby chair for a better view. Bob was leaping from table to table, trying to dodge the five zombies as he reloaded his shotgun. He'd blasted away parts of their limbs, heads, and bodies, but he'd only just slowed them down. Even the one who'd lost both its lower legs and all of one arm was hopping around on stumped thighs, gamely trying to grab Bob's ankles.

Bob turned his head toward the badger. "A little help here?" he called. His voice came through the iBook's speaker a half-second after I heard it through the door.

I leaped the badger onto Runs On Stumps. As the badger bit into the back of its neck, the zombie went rigid, and its skin went white and ashy. The zombie's NecroNulled flesh crumbled like clay beneath the badger's teeth and raking claws.

"Good one!" Bob said. "The others won't go so quick 'cause they ain't hurt so bad."

I attacked the next zombie, which had only a superficial shotgun wound to its shoulder. As the badger's teeth sank into its neck, the zombie roared and punched the badger into a pile of empty computer cases. I heard a dull snap from the speaker, and the badger shuddered.

The screen flashed:

WARNING! SPINAL TAP IN PROGRESS!
Kombat mode not possible. Continue via IKnowKungFu? (Y/N)

Fire! Fire! Fire! my inner teen chanted.

I hit the "Y" key, and the screen went red. The badger rose up, up in the air and floated against the ceiling, scanning for targets. The zombie who'd fractured the badger's spine was flaking apart like asbestos, and the remaining three had cornered Bob, whose shotgun had apparently jammed.

Then Bob looked up, saw the badger, mouthed *Oh crap* and dropped to the floor, covering his head.

The badger screamed down on the zombies, jaws snapping and paws clawing faster than the computer could track. It went clear through one zombie's head like a fuzzy buzzsaw and ripped through the others. I caught a glimpse of Bob crawling desperately for cover at the back of the store. The badger dove in and out, faster and faster, like a small furry dead Superman.

WARNING! OVERLOAD IMMINENT!

I gave the iBook the four-finger salute, but the program was locked. I was just about to hit the power button when the badger exploded.

You know how matter can turn into energy? I found out later that the reason NecroNull is buried in FleshGolem's options is that when IKnowKungFu sparks a spiritual overload, it causes all of the still-living matter in the golem to become energy. A few bacterial cells, usually, or maybe a dying roundworm. Not enough to match the power of a nuclear weapon, but plenty to create one hell of a bang.

Is it a bug, or a feature? I guess it depends on how many zombies you have to kill, and how badly you want them gone.

The boom rocked the entire building, and I was knocked flat. The iBook clattered onto the dirty floor, its keyboard popping free and its screen blacking out.

I got to my feet and cautiously opened the door. Bob lay in an unconscious heap against the back door. The computer shop was a complete wreck. Smoke and zombie blood hung in a thick, rust-red mist. The remaining windows were shattered, and the front door had been blown off its hinges. There was not a single zombie in sight.

Two middle-aged women in pink beautician's smocks stood on the sidewalk outside, squinting into the dark shop. One clutched a Mossberg shotgun. Though their faces and smocks were smudged with soot and blood, their bouffants were immaculate.

"Are you okay in there?" the older of the two women called.

"I'm fine, but Bob needs an ambulance," I replied. "Does the phone in your shop still work?"

"Shore does. I'll go give the boys at 't VFD a holler," she said.

It took me three days to get back to civilization. I didn't end up killing my editor; when I got back we had what diplomats call "a frank and cordial exchange" and, well, we parted ways. After that, I did what any good American would do: I sued.

But all's well that ends well. I used my settlement proceeds to start up the Critter Karaoke Club, and the college kids can't get enough.

The House That Couldn't Clean Itself

Marsha Petrie shuffled through the frosty fall leaves clogging the streets toward the old Victorian rental on Findley Avenue. The moon shone hard and bright above the trees. Her earpiece chimed, and she touched the button on the chilly temple of her smart glasses to answer the call. A webcam image popped up in the corner of her field of vision: her girlfriend Olivia's sleepy face grinning through a cascade of loose brown curls.

"Hey, Marsh, you get in from Vermont okay?"

Marsha smiled in spite of the cold numbing her cheeks. "Yeah, bus dropped me off a couple of minutes ago. Sorry I didn't call. Thought you might be asleep. Didn't wanna wake you."

Olivia's grin turned impish. "Want me to come over and warm you up?"

"Oh, I'd love that…but I stink of Greyhound right now. Some brodude puked rotgut whiskey and pumpkin spice donuts all down the aisle three hours ago."

Olivia stuck out her tongue and wrinkled her nose. "Ewwww!"

"I know, right? So I need a shower and fresh clothes, at least. And I'm dying for a grilled cheese."

"How can you *possibly* still feel like eating after that?" Marsha shrugged.

"It's a talent. But all I've had all day was stuff from bus stop vending machines. I'm done with Doritos for at least a month."

"Was the food at your grad school residency decent, at least?"

"Some stuff was okay. Lots of meatloaf and squash. The cafeteria ladies try, but…"

Olivia finished her thought: "…dorm food is dorm food?"

"Yup." Marsha reached the concrete steps leading up to the house and began to ascend.

"So get a shower, and let's hit Steak 'n Shake."

"It'll be at least 2 a.m. before I'm ready."

"I don't have to be up early tomorrow; do you?"

"No, but…ugh, I have to pay my tuition installment next week." Marsha reached the front porch and stomped the snow off her boots. "I should at least attempt to be frugal. I put cheese and bread in the freezer before I left, so I can make my own sandwich."

"Assuming those losers you live with didn't eat your food."

"Be nice." She shrugged out of her blue backpack and set it down on the snowy worn boards to dig out her house key. With the aid of vacuum bags and careful clothing choices, she'd once used it as her sole luggage for a 10-day trip to Canada. Subsequently, her friends had nicknamed the pack the Tardis.

"Ain't nothing but nice, girlfriend. Just making a completely factual observation."

"*Anyway.*" She wasn't in the mood to badmouth her housemates. She'd only been in the house for a week before she'd had to leave for her residency, and the girl she'd sublet her room from *had* seemed very, very eager for Marsha to move in, but she chalked it up to the girl having just landed a job in Chicago. Marsha would have been anxious at the prospect of having to pay double rent, too, and equally thrilled to avoid it. Jake, Marco, Brandon and Steve were computer science students at Ohio State and all seemed like decent enough guys. A person just had to be tolerant of personality quirks in a shared living arrangement. If the guys were willing to overlook her occasional compulsion to binge on her shows at 3 a.m., she could overlook their eccentricities, too.

Marsha unlocked the front door. "I also need to attempt to have something resembling an adult sleep schedule, even if all my classes are online and whenever."

Olivia sighed. "I feel you. I should be better about that myself. How about you come over tomorrow after you wake up and I can make us lunch?"

"Deal." She pushed the door open and flipped on the lamp…then swore long and hard.

Olivia frowned in concern. "What's the matter?"

"Look at this!" Marsha toggled her glasses camera's view to display the dimly lit living room. It had been a bit dusty and cluttered with random books and gaming accessories when she'd left. But now? It looked like FedEx and Amazon had waged a terrifying battle in the room. The floor was thick with packing peanuts, shreds of bubble wrap, and wads of brown paper padding. Empty shipping boxes of every size lay tossed about like slaughtered cardboard soldiers—she noted that the guys now had a brand-new 80-inch frameless multidimensional curvescreen mounted on the wall, which *Doctor Who* was going to look *amazing* on—and all the tables were stacked high with games and books and movies and action figures and other random geekanalia. The only clear place in the whole room was the couch in front of the TV.

"You better check the kitchen," Olivia stage-whispered.

Marsha closed the door, set her backpack down on a relatively clear patch of floor, and began to pick her way through the debris.

"Duuuh-nuh! Duuuh-nuh!" Olivia sang the theme to *Jaws* inside her ear.

"Oh, stop. How bad could it be after just one week?" Marsha hopped over a box into the kitchen and flipped on the light.

"*This bad,*" Olivia intoned as Marsha sucked in her breath.

If the living room looked like a battleground, the kitchen was nothing short of Apocalypse incarnate. Dried, marinara-crusted spaghetti spattered the floor and walls. The stovetop was spackled an inch thick with more marinara, soup, chili, toast crumbs, cheese, and God knew what else. And the dishes. Sweet Jesus, the dishes. A Mount Doom of dirty pots, pans, plates, and cups rose from the moldy sink higher than her head and spread in a fester of filthy glassware across the entire counter.

To top it off, a pizza-sized splotch dripped red, greasy stalactites from the ceiling. Part of her admired the precise aim involved in getting such even coverage, but the rest of her was horrified.

"How?" Marsha croaked. "It was not like this when I left, I swear!"

"Clearly, they suckered that last girl into cleaning up their shit for them." Olivia shook her head, disgusted. "And she suckered *you* into taking her place."

Marsha felt faint. She could not make a sandwich in here. She couldn't even find enough space to pour a glass of milk. Heck, she didn't want to consume food or beverages that had been *opened* in here. "I. Cannot. Even…I. *Will. Not.*"

"Did they eat your cheese, too?"

Marsha went to the freezer and opened it. It was empty except for a couple of sports gel packs and an ice cube tray. "Yes. Dammit, they did."

"Okay, this is a serious situation and it deserves a serious, face-to-face discussion," Olivia said. "Meet me at the Steak 'n Shake in fifteen minutes!"

"For the record, you don't smell nearly as badly as you think you do." Olivia waved a shoestring French fry at Marsha. "In fact, I can't smell you at all."

"That's good." She shifted, still feeling uncomfortably unwashed under the bright lights of the diner, and absently watched the gleaming round chrome vacbot hoover up crumbs and spilled fries from the white-and-black checkered floor.

"So, as your lawyer and your girlfriend—"

"Wait, you're not a lawyer." Marsha countered.

"I just took a course on contract law," Olivia replied.

Marsha squinted. "That's really not the same, though."

Olivia scowled comically and gave herself a fry moustache and a fake British accent. "Harrumph! I say, look here, young lady, do you want my advice or nay?"

"Of course I do."

She ate her frystache. "Okay, so as your girlfriend who just scored an A in contract law, thank you very much, I say you break that stupid sublease you signed and move in with me and Rachel."

"I'm not comfortable with that," Marsha replied, watching carbonation bubbles fight for the surface against the ice cubes in her cherry limeade. "I don't want to break a lease. She could sue me, right?"

"She could, but first, this is pretty clearly a case of fraud on her part. If she didn't use the words 'filthy schmilthy dirthole', then she hid important living conditions from you. And second, your sublease is up in four months anyhow, right? So she'd have to be willing to lawyer up to go after you over a few months of rent. If she's busy, it'll be easier to just eat the money and move on."

"I dunno…it still seems like a crappy thing to do."

"What's crappy is tricking somebody into signing a lease for a pig-pit with no warning. Look, I helped you move in…I *know* you don't have that much stuff. It'll fit in our place, no problem, and then we can upgrade to a bigger apartment in the spring. We could get you moved out of there tomorrow."

Olivia wistfully dipped her fries in ketchup. "It's a shame we're both in old rentals nobody's going to modernize. All the new high-end condos they're building downtown come with options for automated cleaning systems. Leave a plate on the counter overnight, and the condo puts it in the dishwasher. They've got self-sanitizing kitchen sinks, and bathrooms that can move your stuff out of the way to clean and then put it back. You can just live in your home and not worry about anything but the mortgage. Those systems are *super* expensive, but they'd be *so* nice."

"They do sound really cool." Marsha watched the patrolling vacbot suck up an errant straw wrapper. "Maybe we could just get a robot and solve this whole problem?"

"A robot?" Olivia followed her gaze. "Oh, that little thing would *die* in there. And it couldn't solve the dishes problem."

"No, not a bot like this one," Marsha replied. "I'm talking one of the hotel-grade android models."

"What? Those are crazy expensive, too!"

Marsha pulled out her tablet and tapped 'cleaning droid rental prices Columbus, OH' into her web search. "They're not so bad if you rent them, though. See?"

She showed the results to Olivia, who looked unconvinced. "That's still a lot."

"That's less than they're paying for their media service bundle. And they just bought that cool-ass TV. Clearly they have money from *somewhere*. I just have to convince them to spend it on something they haven't cared about."

Olivia gave her a hard look. "Are you really so dead-set against living with me that you're going to continue living with these filthy buffoons and rent a robot instead? Don't you love me?"

A sudden shock of realization bolted through Marsha. This whole conversation was way more serious than she'd guessed. She had to speak with utmost care, or she was going to lose something worth far more than a few months of rent.

"I do love you. Of *course* I love you," Marsha replied, her mind racing to analyze possible stupidity before she spoke it aloud. "It's just that I've seen so many relationships wreck after couples move in together. We've *both* seen it. Julia and Sam, Bo and Rick, Mary and Tony…they all moved in and broke up just months afterward."

"But a lot of people stayed together." Tears shone in Olivia's eyes. "Mia and Josie are still together. And more, but I don't have a *catalog of failure* memorized like you do."

Suddenly the diner seemed too small, too stuffy. The teenagers giggling in the booths around them seemed to be mocking her idiocy. The embarrassed panic building in her chest made her want to bolt into the ladies' room and hide.

Instead, she reached out across the table and took Olivia's warm hands in hers.

"I love you more than anything, and I don't want to lose you. If…if you *really* want me to move in with you, okay, yes, let's do that. *Immediately.* But it just seems like a huge hassle for both of us right now with all the classwork we have to do. It seems like it would be so much simpler if I could just ride things out where I am until winter break. And I *did* sign a contract."

Marsha took a deep breath. "I *signed* it. Even if you think I can just skip out on it, the idea of breaking my word over something fixable just doesn't sit right. Someone just needs to clean the house, and it'll be fine! And I couldn't afford to pay you a fair share of my costs if I'm still paying for the sublease. I don't want to be a burden on you, not even for a few months."

Olivia wiped her eyes on a paper napkin. "You wouldn't be a burden, but… okay. All that makes sense, I guess. But what if they don't go for the robot? Are you just going to live with the filth?"

Marsha shook her head. "No. I can't live with it. And I'm going to make that clear to them. They'll go for the robot. They'll *have* to."

They went back to Olivia's place afterwards to take a shower and make love. While Olivia snoozed, Marsha slipped out of bed, went to the futon in the spartan living room, and sat bathed in the blue glow of her tablet, intently building a proposal for her housemates.

"Bow down before my PowerPoint, mortals," Marsha muttered as she assembled statistics and robot performance details as mentally delicious to gadget geeks as any chocolate-covered bonbons. She didn't know her new housemates well, but she intuited that they were just like her in one important way: weak for sexy new hardware, be it computers or gaming systems. A robot—even one designed for something as mundane as dusting and vacuuming and washing up—would be no different. She just had to keep her text upbeat and focused on the sweet new toy they'd have in their house.

And it would be the sweetest toy they'd ever had. "We're getting a freakin' *robot*!"

Ultimately, she pitched them two rental models that both had very good online reviews: the iRobot HouseBuddy, which was a stocky, multi-armed robot that resembled R2D2 from *Star Wars*, and the CoreBotics MeriMaid, which was an android with exaggerated feminine curves, cartoon red lips, and arms that ended in a variety of attachments. She felt a little uncomfortable for suggesting the MeriMaid because to her eye it was sexist as hell. But on the other hand, if they thought of cleaning as being women's work—and evidence so far indicated that they did—then they'd be more likely to go for the sexy-looking femmebot than the R2 knockoff. Marsha was okay with feeling a bit dirty if it meant the house got clean.

She emailed her proposal to all her housemates just after 4 a.m., turned off notifications on her tablet and glasses, and crawled back into Olivia's bed.

They both woke up around noon, and Olivia made them coffee and eggs while Marsha checked the email thread that had exploded while she slept.

"How does it look?" Olivia asked.

"The good news is, nobody's arguing against getting a robot," Marsha replied. "They're totally down with a robot."

"And the bad news…?"

"They're arguing over what model to get. There's kind of a *lot* of arguing. So this does me no good if they can't actually get around to making a decision."

"Play hard ball," Olivia said. "Threaten to leave if they don't get a robot by tomorrow."

Another email popped up and her tablet emitted a bloop.

"What's that?" Olivia set the coffee pot down on a silicone trivet on the dining table.

"Email from my housemate Brandon. He says, and I quote, 'Robots? Those are more like total blowbots. I can get a better robot from my cousin at Carolina Mechatronics. Gimme a couple of days.'"

"Doesn't that company mostly make stuff for the Department of Defense?" Olivia asked.

"Yeah. Yeah, they do." Marsha started tapping in her reply. "I'm asking for a clarification."

She sent her message and mixed cream and sugar into her coffee. A few minutes later Brandon's reply arrived.

"What does he say?" Olivia asked.

"He says, 'My cousin can hook me up with one of their beta android models. I can download a Torrent of standard cleaning routines and reprogram it, no sweat. It'll be able to do anything that stupid MeriMaid model can do, *and* we can enter it into the battlebots tourney on campus.'"

"Battlebots. Um." Olivia flipped the eggs over, looking pained. "As your girlfriend and lawyer, I advise you to move anything breakable to this apartment, just in case."

Marsha spent the next several days eating most meals at Olivia's house but she slept at the Findley Avenue house on general principle; after all, she was paying for it. She cleaned the bathroom she shared with Marco out of sheer necessity, but steered clear of the kitchen.

But on the sixth morning, she awoke to the pinging of an urgent message.

Marsha put on her glasses and followed a link to a 3D video feed of the OSU open maker lab. Brandon was wearing goggles and a white lab coat, standing in a triumphant Superman pose. His unwashed brown hair stuck up in mad scientist peaks. Someone—presumably Brandon—had set up a crude living room replica with an inflatable red loveseat, a battered lamp on a crate, and a scattering of sawdust and metal shards on a section of old carpet.

"The XC930B arrived yesterday, and I've repainted him and uploaded his new programming. Check it out!" He turned to his left. "ExCee, activate!"

A tall, blocky android painted candy apple red with silver-and-yellow flames stomped into the video frame. Clearly, whoever made this machine had built it to intimidate. The shoulders were nearly as wide as a doorway and armored with heavy riveted pauldrons. The face was a smooth, featureless chrome visor. Very little about it other than its bipedal shape implied any sort of humanity.

"ExCee, clean!" ordered Brandon.

The android saluted him with a slablike hand.

"Sanitation commencing!" it boomed in a raspy synthesized voice.

Telescoping fingers collapsed into the hand, and the hand retracted into its wrist. A split-second later, a metal rod emerged that blossomed into bristles: a broom, Marsha realized. The bulky robot moved with surprising quickness and grace as it swept the debris on the rug into a neat pile. Its other hand transformed into a black nozzle, and it vacuumed up the dust and shards as deftly as a conductor silencing a symphony.

Grinning, Brandon spread his hands wide. "Does he rock, or does he *rock*?"

Looks good! Marsha messaged him. *When will he be ready?*

Brandon glanced down at her text on the face of his smart watch. "Two days. Three days, tops."

She disconnected from the video feed, put on her robe, and went downstairs into the kitchen. It was even worse than before. She wasn't sure how anyone had any room to do any cooking, but there were yet more spatters on the floor and walls. Seemingly every single pot, plate and glass was dirty, but instead of doing dishes, her roommates had opted to buy disposables instead. The black rubber industrial-grade trashcan beside the fridge was overflowing with red Solo cups and discarded paper plates.

Her hands itched just looking at it. She could clean it. None of it was her mess, but she *could* make it go away. It would only take her most of the day, and she'd need to buy gloves and a filter mask and bleach first. And the whole kitchen would be just as nasty the following Sunday.

No. She would not. The robot would be there that weekend, and he would put things right.

"Soon," she whispered to the filth. "Very soon."

She got another video message from Brandon that Sunday morning.

"Prepare yourselves!" Brandon looked ecstatic. "XC930B is ready and I'm bringing him home from the maker lab right now!"

Marsha quickly dressed and went downstairs. Her other roommates were lounging on couches and boxes, drinking Mountain Dews and playing the new Metroid racing game. She heard the clomp of steel boots on cold concrete steps, and a few seconds later Brandon pushed into the house with his flashy red robot in tow.

"Daaang!" breathed Steve.

"He's totally bad-ass!" Jake exclaimed.

Marco looked the mighty android up and down. "Does he do windows?"

"Screw the windows. Can he do the kitchen?" Marsha asked.

Brandon gave her a wide smile, and for the first time she suspected he might have a bit of a thing for her. And that suspicion made her glad she'd only have to live with him for a few more months. Even if he'd been a girl, she found his oblivious hyperactivity exhausting and wouldn't have wanted to date him.

"ExCee, sanitize the kitchen!" Brandon ordered.

The robot saluted him and clomped through the living room. Marsha and her roommates followed after him, crowding in the doorway to see what would happen.

XC930B stood in the middle of the kitchen and began to scan everything with an oscillating green laser. Suddenly, a bright red alarm light began flashing behind its visor.

"Biohazards detected! Biohazards detected!" the robot blared. "*Salmonella, Listeria, Clostridium*, vancomycin resistant *Enterococcus* bacteria and *Stachybotrys* mold detected! Initiating emergency mitigation procedure KIWF1!"

Everyone scrambled back from the doorway.

"What's happening?" Marsha yelled at Brandon.

He looked profoundly confused. "I—I don't—"

FWOOOSH!

The robot's right arm had transformed into a flamethrower and it was hosing down the teetering pile of filthy dishes and overflowing trashcan with what Marsha could only guess was napalm. She'd never imagined that fire could gush like that. The vinyl mini-blinds over the kitchen sink shriveled and blackened, and the windowpane and drinking glasses cracked and shattered in the intense heat. Clouds of noxious smoke poured from the fire.

"No!" shrieked Brandon. "Bad robot! Stop! BAD ROBOT!"

The robot did not stop.

After she'd contacted 911 through her glasses, Marsha stood on the other side of the street from the rental house and called Olivia.

"So, this happened." Marsha showed her the house, which was now entirely engulfed in orange flames. Somewhere in the back yard, muffled by the crackling of the roof collapsing, she could hear Brandon still screaming "Bad robot!"

"Ho. Lee. Shit." Olivia breathed.

"Everybody's okay, I think. I got out through the upstairs fire escape. I was able to grab my wallet, Tardis, tablet bag and coat, but the rest of my stuff is probably toast," Marsha said, feeling numb. "On the plus side, I guess that black mold situation in the kitchen isn't a problem anymore. Nor, it would seem, is my sublease."

"Oh, honey."

"Mind if I crash at your place?"

"Of *course* not." Olivia's tone made it clear that Marsha had just asked the silliest of silly questions.

A lump rose in Marsha's throat. "I love you."

"I love you too. Now get your butt over here and let me take you clothes shopping. We can pick you up a costume for the party next weekend while we're out…."

After Hours

There once was a Halloween book
And you, Dear Reader, took a look!
If you've enjoyed these tales so far,
Beware! The final two are Rated R!
(I'd *never* want you to be shook.)

The Toymaker's Joy

Hildrina the Elf was busy filling a fleecy white teddy bear with the softest cotton batting when she felt her supervisor's gentle touch on her shoulder.

"Hildy." Sanjeeta's voice was pleasant as always but carried a faint note of warning that might as well have been a full-blown klaxon of doom as far as the junior elf was concerned.

Hildrina quickly set down the teddy bear lest her sudden dread and sweaty palms taint the toy. "Yes?"

"Do you have a moment to come to my office? I just wanted to go over recent QA results with you."

"Of course." Heart pounding, Hildrina pushed away from the ancient oak workbench and followed Sanjeeta to her office. Was it her imagination that the other elves' eyes were upon her? Judging her? She felt herself blush, wishing the office weren't clear at the other end of the workshop and that getting there didn't have this terrible Walk of Shame feel to it.

Hildrina made herself hold her head high and look squarely at the green satin ribbon decorating the long glossy black braid trailing down the center of her supervisor's back. Anyone who got promoted to Stuffed Animals was a skilled toymaker. She was just as good as anyone else in the workshop. She wouldn't get sent back to Tags & Bags. She *wouldn't*. If she had messed up somehow, surely there would be a way to fix it.

"Please have a seat." Her supervisor gestured toward the comfy padded chair in front of her desk as she pulled the door closed behind them. The pumpkin-shaped bells on the Halloween wreath decorating the door jangled as the latch clicked shut. Sanjeeta's desk was bare except for two stuffed toys Hildrina had recently made: a plush tiger and a baby seal. Both looked fine as far as the junior elf could see.

Hildrina sat, eyeing the toys, trying to surreptitiously wipe her palms off on her striped red tights. She decided she might as well take the reindeer by the horns. "Is…is there a problem with my work, ma'am?"

Sanjeeta sat behind the desk, smiling as always but her eyes looked troubled. "*Problem* is perhaps too strong a word. We do realize you're quite new to this workshop and we want you to do well here."

Hildrina tried to still her pounding heart. "I want to do well. I want that very much, ma'am."

"We know that. All your past supervisors have remarked on your work ethic and your drive to become a top toymaker. And on a technical level, your work is without fault. Your seams are tight and straight, your small parts attachments are completely toddler-proof, and you have an excellent eye for good fabric combinations."

Sanjeeta took a deep breath, clearly steeling herself to give Hildrina some bit of uncomfortable bad news. "But as you know, what we do here isn't just a craft. It's an art. It's *magic*. We are certainly not running an assembly line sweatshop here, you understand?"

"Yes, ma'am. Of course."

"Your toys, while technically flawless, lack the required spirit. Frankly, they feel a little sleepy."

So what? Hildrina found herself thinking. Her toys were going to go to some little boy or girl someplace who'd cuddle them as they went to bed. Sleepy couldn't be a bad thing, could it?

But Sanjeeta was staring at her, clearly expecting some kind of response, so Hildrina said, "I guess maybe I've been a little sleepy lately and that's been affecting my work. I will try to do better."

Hildrina had been sleepy a whole lot in recent weeks because she'd been working late at night in the Joylab, but she knew better than to tell her supervisor that. Elves were allowed to work after hours in the lab as long as it didn't affect their regular duties. This was obviously a clear-cut case of work interference.

Sanjeeta pursed her lips. "I'm getting the feeling that you don't fully understand the importance of imbuing the proper spirit in your work. Which isn't surprising. There are…details about the toys that we don't usually share with crafters."

Her supervisor inflected the word "details" with such portent that Hildrina's breath caught in her throat. What details? What could she mean?

"If I understood the situation better, I think I could do a better job," she offered.

"If I tell you," Sanjeeta replied, "you have to promise that you won't speak of this with anyone else."

"I swear I won't." Hildrina held up her hand in a promissory salute. "I swear on my honor as an elf of Clan Kandyflöss."

"Okay, then." Sanjeeta smiled and held up the tiger and seal that Hildrina crafted. "What do you think will happen to these toys?"

"They'll become Christmas presents, of course."

"Not of course. *Never* assume that the work we do here is just for Christian children," Sanjeeta said. "Our duty is to *all* children, regardless of their families' faiths or lack thereof."

Hildrina felt an ashamed heat rise in her face. "Of course, ma'am."

"Don't be embarrassed. It was a bit of a trick question." She paused. "Do you remember the spirit instructions that came with the orders for these two toys?"

"Comfort…and bravery?"

"Yes, exactly those."

Sanjeeta held up the seal. "This little creature will go straight to the gift shop of Children's Hospital in Columbus, Ohio. The mother of a five-year-old girl with cancer will buy it for her daughter right before the little girl has to go into an isolation unit because her immune system has collapsed. This toy you made will be her only comfort during those long days and nights when she's in pain and terribly sick and can't feel her mother's touch. This toy you made needs to help give her the bravery she'll need to battle her illness. I don't doubt that it will help her sleep, but will it help her fight for her life?"

Hildrina felt a cold shock down to the soles of her feet. "I…I don't know."

Sanjeeta set down the seal and held up the tiger. "This toy will go to a shop in Syria. A seven-year-old boy will see it and fall in love. His mother will buy it for him. Three days later, bombs will fall and he'll be trapped in the wreckage of their apartment. He'll have nothing but this tiger to keep him brave in the darkness and dust."

Tears welled in Hildrina's eyes. "Will the children live?"

Sanjeeta set down both toys. "I don't know. But I do know that they'll have to be very, very brave to survive. And these toys, these constructions of plush and cotton, these are their shields against the horrors in their lives. When their parents are gone, when they can't even see the sun, these toys will be their only companions to keep them strong."

Hildrina couldn't stop herself from weeping. "I didn't make them good enough. I let those kids down. I'm so sorry."

"Shh…there, there." Sanjeeta came around the desk to give Hildrina a gentle hug. "Don't despair! We have a rigorous QA process; the toys will go to Hong and she will imbue them with all the bravery they're missing."

Hildrina sniffled and wiped her eyes on her green velvet sleeve. "So they're not wrecked?"

"Not at all! A well-constructed toy could never be a wreck. But I know it's important to you to become a truly great toymaker, and to do that, you need to put your heart as well as your mind into the work."

Hildrina stared down at her own hands; they trembled with anxiety. "I… I'm really afraid I'm going to screw up now. I…I never knew the toys were so important for the kids."

Sanjeeta sighed and patted the junior elf's shoulder, making the tiny silver bells decorating her tunic collar tinkle. "And *this* is why we usually don't tell the toymakers about where their creations go. That kind of knowledge leads to inhibited performance more often than it leads to performance improvements, I'm afraid."

"I promise I'll do better—" Hildrina began.

"Look," Sanjeeta said. "I really don't want you to get stressed out over this. *Really.* I want you to succeed here at the North Pole, and it could be that the Stuffed Animals Workshop isn't the place where you can truly shine. And there would be no shame in that at all! There are dozens of workshops here, and I don't want to see you limit yourself."

"What do you want me to do?" Hildrina asked.

"For the next couple of days, I just want you to think about things. You can work at your regular bench—know that we'll be giving all your toys an integrity check, and if there's a deficiency anywhere, be confident that we'll catch it and fix it. Or, if you're feeling especially nervous, you can just do eyes or tags or some other kind of focused work for a few days. Sound good?"

Hildrina nodded, still feeling terrible about her failure. "Yes."

"Okay." Sanjeeta gave her a bright smile. "October's only just begun, so let's meet again toward the end of the month. That way, we can be certain you'll be ready for the November crunch."

At dinner, Hildrina was listlessly pushing her roasted butternut squash around her plate with her fork when her friend Freddie plopped down on the bench beside her.

"Hey Hildy! How's the world of teddy bears?" He grinned.

"Ugh. I messed up." She rubbed her temples. "I've been messing up since I got there, apparently."

"What? *You?* How?"

Hildrina glanced at Freddie to make sure he wasn't being sarcastic; his pale, freckled face bore nothing but a genuine expression of surprise and concern.

"I'm not giving the toys the right emotional resonance, I guess," she replied. "And that matters way more than I thought it did."

"Huh." He blinked. "I wouldn't have guessed that."

"Me, neither." She sighed.

"Are you in trouble?"

"Not *trouble* trouble. More like, I really want to do a good job, you know? But I'm not sure I can." She pulled her sleeves down over her hands and shrugged inside her candy-striped shirt. "Not *there*, anyhow. I'm scared that I'll just be… mediocre."

"Well, you could always transfer over to the Diecast Workshop!" Freddie pulled a shiny red toy Porsche out of the pocket of his jerkin and zoomed it across the table. "We have a lot of fun over there."

"I'm not so good with painting, though." She speared a cube of squash on a single fork tine. "You know, I wish I could just work in the Joylab full-time."

"Wouldn't that be a kick? But *nobody* gets to do that. Nobody I've heard of, anyhow. You going after dessert?"

"I've got the new toy curing in its mold; it should be ready to come out," she replied, thinking hard about her priorities. "But if I go, I know I'll be there 'til at least midnight, and then I'll be sleepy again tomorrow…so maybe I just shouldn't go tonight."

"This is the toy you designed yourself, right?"

"Yes, I've been working on it for three months now."

"How can you just let your own toy languish in its mold?" he exclaimed. "You *have* to get it finished and show it to people! I mean, if Coriander thinks it's cool, then at the very least that'll make you feel better about things, right?"

"But what if he *doesn't* think it's cool?" she asked morosely.

"Well, then you just try again with something else, right?" He gave her shoulder a gentle punch. "Let's go get some cider cake and hit the lab.

"Need some help with that?" Freddie asked as Hildrina carefully lifted the leather-strapped mold from the shelf.

"No, I've got it." She set the mold down on her workbench and began to unbuckle the straps. Her heart beat faster. Had the toy cured properly? Would it emerge as beautiful as she imagined, or would it be another misshapen attempt?

The halves of the mold were still tight, so she got a putty knife and wiggled them apart. When they fell away from the toy inside, she and Freddie gasped simultaneously.

The 9-inch gleaming dildo wobbled majestically, a miracle of swirling silver and blues and purples. It was far too big for any elf, but it would be the perfect size and hardness for many humans. But shape and size were the easy parts; it was the aesthetics that had failed in her past prototypes. Hildrina had hoped to capture the mystery and glory of the Horsehead Nebula in the silicone shaft… and she'd finally done it. By Saint Nick, she'd done it!

"Wooow," Freddie breathed. "Can—can I touch it?"

"Sure," she replied.

He gingerly poked the flaring head with his forefinger. "Whoa! It feels real. How did you get the galaxy swirls to move inside it like that?"

"It's got a soft skin layer over gel mid-layer over a stiff silicone core. It's an advance on the Vixskin and Cyberskin models on the market. The colors respond to heat and motion but the toy is still durable enough to be boiled or run through the dishwasher."

"It's so *cool.*"

"Hey, what have you got there?" Coriander came over, a vibrator motor in one hand and a screwdriver in the other. The manager's bushy white brows rose and his eyes widened.

"Oh my sweet candycanes. That…is gorgeous. So beautiful." Twin tears dripped from Coriander's shining eyes. "*It's…it's full of stars!*"

Hildrina blushed and smiled. "Thank you, sir."

"A pity there's no harness to match a toy so wondrous," Coriander said.

"Oh, I made one a few months ago." Hildrina opened the bottom drawer of her workbench and pulled out a glittering purple-black dildo harness. "It's vegan leather, non-toxic, and machine washable!"

Coriander made a high squealing noise that startled Hildrina. "Oh, we must tell the boss! We *must!*"

Hildrina blinked at him. "Like…now? But it's got to be close to his bedtime."

"Yes, this very instant! He will want to see. Oh, he *must* see! An innovation like this could ensure funding for the whole laboratory!"

Coriander rushed off to his office.

Freddie grinned at Hildrina and gently punched her shoulder. Her bells jingled.

"Hildy, you done good!"

Hildrina walked into the echoing presentation chamber, carefully laid the box containing her new toy and harness in the middle of the spotlight illuminating the gleaming wooden floor, and sat down in the only chair, which was facing the wall to make things easier on elves whose creations met with disapproval. It was one thing to hear that the boss didn't like a creation, but it was quite another to see disapproval on his noble face. Apparently one sensitive elf was utterly devastated by what he saw in his master's eyes, so the easiest fix was to turn the chair around.

It was a nicely plush recliner, but its comfort did nothing to soothe her jangling nerves. Her hands trembled, and she was sweating through her tunic despite how cold she felt.

She'd been in this room once before during orientation; she'd never imagined she'd be in here again. It was a rare prototype that was deemed worthy to be presented straight to the boss. What if he didn't like her toy? It wasn't at all for a child, after all. What if he thought it was dirty and terrible? Coriander's hopes were so high now…what if she failed him? What if the boss hated her toy and she failed everybody in the lab?

Her breath caught in her throat as she heard the door swing open. She shut her eyes at the sound of heavy booted feet crossing the floor. She trembled at the sound of tissue paper rustling.

Please like it please like it please like it, she prayed silently.

"Ho ho *ho*." His voice was a rich, rolling basso, the voice of a living god. Her skin prickled with goosebumps. "What do we have here? Most…interesting."

More rustling, and a long silence.

"I believe I should show this to the missus," he finally announced. "This… might take a little while. Did you bring something to occupy yourself?"

"No, sir." Her voice was a reedy, broken whisper.

A sound like a midwinter breeze rustling pine needles rose in the chamber, and suddenly a shiny red Nintendo 3DS dropped into her hands. Tetris was paused on the screen.

"Oh, I love this game!" she exclaimed.

He chuckled low and she got more goosebumps. "I know."

Hildrina woke with a start when the door opened again. What time was it? She'd fallen asleep in an awkward ball in the chair, curled around the closed Nintendo. A small puddle of drool gleamed on the case. She clumsily tried to wipe it off with the hem of her sleeve.

"Hildrina the Elf," Santa Claus rumbled. "Stand and look at me."

"Y-yes sir." She stood up, did her best to straighten her sleep-rumpled clothes, and turned to face the towering master of the North Pole, who was dressed in a deep red bathrobe and white bunny slippers. He smelled like peppermint soap and talcum powder, as if he'd just showered. His face was quite red, his gray eyes fierce.

150

"Was this toy of yours an accident?" he demanded.

She suddenly wished the polished floorboards would open and drop her into an abyss. "N-no, sir. I…I did a lot of research, and I've been working on it a long time."

"So you can create it again?"

"It wouldn't be *exactly* the same, but I can create something very much like it. Maybe…maybe something even better next time."

"Good. Because my lady has made it clear that she will be keeping that toy. Even if she weren't so adamant, I expect it would be awkward to hand it back to you after what it's been through."

She swallowed. "D-did it hold up, sir?"

"Oh, remarkably well. It's…amazing what it can do."

Hildrina thought she might faint. "I'm glad to hear it, sir."

"I have sent instructions to Coriander," he said. "Tomorrow, you shall work full-time in the Joylab. Create as many of your starry wonders as you like, but I do want to see what else that fertile imagination of yours can come up with. Spend some time each week working with Coriander on mechanical toys; he has a real knack for them. I hear that suction for ladies is the latest big thing."

"Thank you, sir, I will." She was filled with the purest joy, and half expected to float up to the ceiling like a child's balloon.

"What do you call it, by the way?"

She blinked. "Sir?"

"The toy. Has it a name?"

"I call it the Galaxxxy Master."

"Hmm." He stroked his snow-white beard. "Not bad. Not bad at all."

The Tingling Madness

As the Indescribable Horror dragged me down into the black waters of the fathomless quarry, I wondered two things. Had I left the coffee maker plugged in, and would our Siberian kitten Chewie bite through the cord again, resulting in a fire that tragically yet ironically caused my husband to die of smoke inhalation as I drowned? How much frog pee was in the quarry water, and how much of it was I inadvertently swallowing as I struggled against the Horror's slippery arms? And how had I gotten myself into this mess in the first place?

Wait. That was at least three things, wasn't it? They say that your ability to count is one of the first functions to abandon you when madness sets in. "They" being people who probably always had fine arithmetic skills. People who never, ever went crazy from boredom at their day jobs. People who never did questionable things on company time to try to keep their brains engaged.

But I'm not one of those people, and that's how I got into this mess.

I knew I was going to get fired from my content editing job at Skewl about a year before it happened. The signs of my impending unemployment loomed obvious as an Arab sorcerer's curses scrawled in fire upon the conference room walls. Our instructional design group had merged with three other departments, and we'd been moved out of our nice, cheerful offices into a windowless cube farm in the basement. Worse, we kept getting shuffled to new bosses. Half my coworkers quit in frustration because of the supervisor we all called Buzzword Bob. Our workload doubled, then tripled. I was taken off all the art, photography and literature courses I'd been hired for and put to the task of building the worst online business courses you can imagine. "Corporate

Governance and Viscerous Control Assessment." "Quantitative & Qualitative Methods for Necropolitan Decision-Making." "Foundations of Forensic Accountancy for Geriatric Allopathy".

I knew I should keep my head down and be a good hive drone. I knew that they were looking for reasons to fire us. I knew that I should not, should *not* give in and read slash fan fiction online during my breaks, and I particularly shouldn't start *writing* slashfic during said breaks. But the relentless tedium and frustration had awoken something terrible inside me and I couldn't stop myself.

So when I went to my supervisor's office for my September one-on-one meeting and she smiled and said, "Why don't we go upstairs for this discussion?" I felt a spike of dread and adrenaline but also no small bit of relief. Finally, it would be over. And then as we walked to the creaky elevator I felt regret. Why hadn't I escalated my job search? Why hadn't I just dropped the hammer myself and quit when most everybody else did? Mysteries of the universe.

My supervisor led me to a glass-walled room where the HR manager sat primly at the big conference table with a folder and papers set before her.

"Please sit down." The HR lady gestured at the chairs on the opposite side of the table.

I did as she asked, and my supervisor took the chair beside her.

Grimacing, the HR lady pushed a paper-clipped stack of pages toward me. "Can you explain this?"

I looked at the pages. It was a printout of "Pinkie Pipes Pomp," the most popular story I'd posted on the FrackYeahFanfic site. In just four days, it had racked up over one thousand "loves." I'd used my RhinoScribe69 pseudonym and had erased the tale from my hard drive, but of course I'd uploaded it through Skewl servers.

I paused. This was my opportunity to lie and say I'd just looked at it out of curiosity, but I was too tired to think of a good excuse and just wanted this to be over.

"Yes, that's a story I wrote on my lunch break."

The HR lady looked shocked that I'd admitted it so easily. Clearly, she had expected embarrassed stammering, or pleading, rather than calm. "Is the Don Pomp character supposed to be President Trump?"

"Well, actually, he's more of a mix of Trump and Nixon with some Grover Cleveland style."

Her eyes grew narrower, her voice shriller. "And Pinkie Dinkie is a rhinoceros?"

I blinked at her. "Well, yes. Of course he is. Don't you watch *My Little Rhino?*"

The HR Lady and my supervisor both stared at me as if I'd suddenly sprouted a second head that was rapping tracks from *Free Willy: The Musical*.

My supervisor spoke low and slow, like salty barbecue: "You wrote a story in which the sitting President of the United States is graphically violated and degraded by a talking rhinoceros?"

I shook my head. "Violation implies non-consent. If you re-read page two, you'll see that this is an entirely consensual power exchange—"

"Enough!" The HR lady's voice shook like the walls of Jericho. "You have flagrantly violated our computing policies. Your employment here is terminated. Security will bring your belongings out to the parking lot. Please give me your badge."

I unclipped it from my belt loop and pushed it across the table to her. "Don't forget my Pinkie Dinkie action figure."

The HR lady shuddered.

I got home two hours later. My husband Pete rolled his wheelchair down the ramp from the upper level living room. "Darling wife! You're home early?"

I set my cardboard box down on the bench by the front door. "Your darling wife messed up and got fired."

"Oh no. I'm so sorry. What now?"

"I find a new job. In the meantime, we better mind our money."

That night, we sat down to look at our recurring expenses, and I found out we were spending over $200 a month on cable television.

"This is insane." I stared at the bill on his laptop screen. "We *have* to cancel."

Pete looked dismayed. "The Internet, too?"

"No, keep the Internet...we're not *barbarians*. And don't worry about missing out on *CSI: Hoboken*. I'll order an antenna."

The device, which advertised a fifty-mile reception range, arrived two days later. It took less than fifteen minutes to stick the big square antenna to the window and thread the long black coaxial cable behind the bookshelves and our entertainment center to our TV. Pete and I watched in rapt attention as the TV's auto-programmer detected the newly available channels. Five channels…ten…twenty…thirty.…

"Forty air channels?" Pete exclaimed. "All this time, we could have been watching forty channels for *free?*"

"Don't get too excited," I warned. "We get the major networks, but I have no idea what these others are. Could be most of them are infomercials."

"Can we surf through to see?"

"Sure."

I helped Pete out of his chair onto the couch. Our kitten Chewie settled between us and began to purr and gnaw on the side seam of Pete's jeans. He never chewed on my jeans; I didn't know whether to feel slighted, or relieved that my pants weren't constantly wet with kitten drool.

The first channels were standard networks. Then we found a classic sci-fi channel, and a war movies and westerns station. After that were some religious channels in English, Spanish, and Somali…and then a channel that showed hooded figures writhing on the floor of some dimly torch-lit cave somewhere. The picture quality was terrible, grainy black-and-white, as if we were seeing a feed from a cheap security camera mounted to the ceiling.

"What is this?" Pete asked. "Is it an indie movie? Some 'found footage' *Blair Witch* kind of thing?"

"I have no idea." I pressed the "Info" button on the remote; this was the Ia! channel.

"Weird," Pete said.

We sat and watched, waiting for a plot, or commercial, or *something* to make sense of what we were seeing. But there was just more writhing, and guttural moaning, and occasional distant chanting in a language I couldn't place.

"Well, okay, then," Pete said. "Next, please?"

The following channel identified itself as HeWillRise, and so of course I thought it would be a Christian broadcast…but it was another monochrome security camera feed. There were no people visible in the frame, just the slow rise and fall of…what? There was sound, but all I could hear was a white noise like the constant rush of ocean waves.

"Is…is that some kind of big lizard?" Pete asked, squinting at the screen. "Or a crocodile? Or an elephant?"

"It looks a little scaly, and wet, but is that some kind of tentacle?" I definitely saw something like a squid's tentacle slowly curling over the reptilian bulk of whatever body part we were seeing. A flank? A leg? It was impossible to know.

"Maybe? Why are they just showing a little part of it? Is it asleep, or floating and dead, or what?"

"It looks like it's breathing." I was starting to hear something like slow inhalations and exhalations under the sound of the ocean surf. So slow that the creature's lungs had to be bigger than school buses. "It's sleeping. Whatever it is."

"Is this some kind of art film?" Pete sounded annoyed but looked freaked out. "Why won't they pan out so we can see the whole thing?"

"Maybe they can't." I felt a sudden chill. "Maybe it's too big."

Pete turned pale. "This is Weird City. Change it, please."

And I wanted to change it…but my hand had gone limp as my job prospects and wouldn't follow my brain's command. I felt…strangely compelled…to keep…watching….

Pete snatched the remote from my fingers and clicked to the next channel, which was showing a Squeez-E-Cheez commercial. The logo in the lower right corner of the screen indicated that this was the Tingler channel. Thrillers, maybe? *Anything* was an improvement.

"Thank you," I muttered.

The commercial ended, and suddenly we were watching a man dressed like a gold coin humping a well-built naked man in a British pub. Their naughty bits were pixilated out. Pete emitted a high-pitched squeal of dismay that scared Chewie off the couch. The kitten fled, leaving a wispy nimbus of shed fur hanging in the air.

"What in the name of hot buttered buns *is* this?" he exclaimed.

"I…I don't," I began, then stopped, recognition dawning. "Holy crap. I know this. This is 'Pounded By The Pound: Turned Gay By The Socioeconomic Implications Of Britain Leaving The European Union'!"

Pete blinked. "What?"

"Um. It's a short story by Chuck Tingle."

His look of confusion turned profound. "Who?"

"He's an erotica author. He writes about billionaires getting seduced by jet planes and T-rexes and yetis and stuff. His story 'Space Raptor Butt Invasion' got nominated for a Hugo Award."

"Do a lot of his stories have 'butt' in the title?"

"Oh, absolutely."

Pete looked pained, but didn't try to switch back to the safety of major network programming. Now, onscreen, the man/coin lovemaking had created some kind of lightning-rimmed portal into the past so that they could change Britain's vote to leave the EU. About half the dialog was bleeped out.

"Well, this isn't *terrible*," Pete remarked. "But it's certainly more butt-centric than I'm comfortable with."

The movie ended, and a call-in talk show entitled "Voidwatch" began. An actor who called himself Budd Hardmann hosted it. He had apparently worked as a stunt double for Adam Sandler until an accident on-set gave him a near-death vision of a place he called the Void.

"The masters of the Void are always looking for ways into Earth from other timelines and dimensions," Hardmann earnestly told the camera. "And we all have to stay hard to stop them. Good buckaroos always keep their eyes open and their buds close by. Watch for the signs, and if you see something, say something. Caller number one, you're on the air…."

The first caller was Nayad from Madison, Wisconsin, and her voice was tight with fear. "Mr. Hardmann, I'm a long-time viewer and this is my third call to you. The Dreamer is definitely waking up. Anyone can see it. He rolled over just yesterday! I'm so scared about what's going to happen."

"Fear is the fresh-maker, Nayad. And you can use his name."

"I don't want to use his name!"

"That's okay, Nayad. You do you. And I know you're a good ladybuck and you can be strong."

"But what do we do?" she pleaded.

"He can't wake up unless his followers all complete their rituals. Watch for the signs; call us for help if you think something is going on near your town. We can send buckaroos to back you up. Call us any time, day or night."

A toll-free number started flashing at the bottom of the screen. I grabbed a pen and bill envelope off the coffee table and jotted it down.

Pete gave me a supercilious side-eye. "You're taking this seriously? Really?"

"I…I don't know." I squirmed on the couch, embarrassed but remembering how I'd felt watching the strange security cam channels. "*Something* weird is going on."

"All these bizarro channels are probably part of the same multiplex run by the same broadcast company." He gestured dismissively at the TV screen. "It's just huckster showmanship to get viewers hooked on some imaginary supernatural conspiracy, can't you see that?"

"I guess…."

He sighed in exasperation. "If you do call these people, for God's sake don't give them your real name, or address. *Or* your credit card number."

I felt small and stupid, but I couldn't shake my conviction that I'd seen something real. Something that called me to action. Even if I didn't know what the heck it was. "Okay."

"Good."

He flipped the TV back to CBS, and we watched his shows until he got sleepy.

"I'm not tired yet, honey," I said. "Please go to bed without me."

"All right, but don't stay up too late."

After I'd heard him shut the bedroom door and I saw that he'd turned off his bedside light, I switched back to the Ia! channel. This time, the feed showed figures clad in hooded Hello Kitty bathrobes holding hands around some kind of odd geometric shape painted on a dingy basement floor. It had the look of a rehearsal rather than a real ritual, and that made me feel marginally better.

I spent most of the night flipping between Ia!, HeWillRise, and Tingler, trying to get a better sense of what was going on in this strange new world I'd discovered within our own. I learned a couple of things. First, Ia! switched to a different feed every hour on the hour. And second, Budd Hardmann never seemed to sleep; his live show was on every four hours between commercials for cheese and cheese products and short movies based on Chuck Tingle stories.

I called the talk show number just after midnight, and the operator put me through to Hardmann.

"Hello, caller number three, you're on the air. Can you give us your status, name and location?"

"New viewer, first-time caller, and I prefer to remain anonymous for now." My voice echoed through the TV speakers.

"That's okay; you do you. What's your question or concern?"

"My husband believes that your channel, the Ia! channel, and HeWillRise are all part of the same multiplex. Run by the same people."

"No, ma'am," Hardmann shook his head vehemently. "Ia! and HeWillRise are a duoplex, and we are independents using the power of love against their devil ways. We are Templars to their vampires, Spongebob to their Plankton."

"But why would Ia! and HeWillRise show what they show?" I persisted. "Wouldn't it make way more sense to be covert about trying to take over the world?"

"Have you watched HeWillRise?"

I paused, staring at the ceiling. "Yes."

"And didn't you feel compelled to keep watching?"

"Yes. I did."

"That's how they get you. Most humans can't look at Cthulhu for more than a minute or two before they feel the call of the Void. And then, if they can tear themselves away, they flip over to Ia! and think, hey, that looks like fun. I should join in the dance. Boogie down for the Apocalypse. Those channels are traps, like diet soda when you're trying to lose weight."

"But I don't want to join in the dance," I said. "I want to stop the music."

"Stay hard, anonymous ladybuck," Hardmann said. "The forces of love need you. When it's time, you'll know."

I spent the next several nights watching Ia! and Tingler after Pete went to bed.

The sleep deprivation was starting to make the world feel unreal, like everything around me was just a painted set, but I couldn't stop myself.

And then, on the fifth night, it happened: I was watching Ia! when the feed switched to figures in hooded rain ponchos cavorting around ritual scrawlings on a pebbled beach. And I recognized it: Murkstone was an old limestone quarry that had been abandoned when the mining crew broke through into an undetected aquifer back in the 1950s. The whole thing filled up with water in a matter of hours. The rumor was the aquifer went down for miles, and that's why the authorities forbade swimming in it. Which of course didn't stop any of the local teens from going skinny-dipping. I'd gone there lots in high school.

The feed was pretty grainy, but I was *sure* it was Murkstone.

Mostly sure, anyway. There was only one way to be absolutely sure.

So, of course, an hour later I was crouched down in the damp grass behind some leaf-bare bushes staring at wet cultists through the gaps in the brush. There wasn't a set, or a TV crew, just a security cam and laptop sitting on a rock. Yep. I was absolutely, 100% sure.

I eased my phone out of my pocket and dialed the Voidwatch number.

"Someone who knows what they're doing needs to come out here," I told the operator. "I'm at Murkstone Quarry in Central Ohio, and there is definitely a cult ritual going on out here."

"We'll send backup," the young man replied. "Can you give me the address?"

"Yes, it's at the corner of Highway 42 North and French Lick Road."

"Can I get your name?"

I paused, remembering my promise to Pete, and then gave him the first pseudonym that popped into my head. "I'm RhinoScribe69."

"Did you write 'Pinkie Pipes Pomp' for FrackYeahFanfic?" the operator asked. I blinked, startled. "Um, yes?"

"Oh my stars, I *loved* that story!" he gushed. "Everybody here loved it! What you did to expand Pinkie Dinkie's childhood backstory was nothing short of brilliant! And his domination of Don Pomp was amazing. The sociopolitical metaphor…just brilliant!"

I felt my cheeks grow hot in the cool air. "Thank you. You're much too kind. But, you know, the cult is doing their thing, and maybe someone could stop them?"

"Absolutely," he assured me. "I'll send a dispatch ASAP. Stay hard!"

Rough hands grabbed the back of my windbreaker. I screamed like a five-year-old and dropped my cell phone. They jerked me to my feet and spun me around. I was facing two scowling cultists in matching scarlet-and-gray Buckeye Football rain ponchos. They were both built like major household appliances and outweighed me by at least seventy-five pounds apiece.

"Looks like we got a spy, Kevin," one growled to the other.

"And you know what happens to spies 'round here."

They gave me meaningful stares, and an awkward silence reigned.

"Actually, I don't know what happens to spies," I said.

"They get to meet the Indescribable Horror," not-Kevin growled.

"I really don't think that's necessary," I protested as they dragged me up the trail and onto the pebbled beach.

They planted me in front of a slender man of medium height who wore a fancy silk maroon robe embroidered with curvilinear symbols in gold thread. He was about thirty years old, and had short russet hair styled up into a rain-damp fauxhawk. One of his eyes was hazel, and the other a pale sky blue. They both bulged slightly, and something about his gaze reminded me of a tree frog. His thin, angular face was dusted with freckles, and he had a tattoo of Abe Vigoda on the left side of his neck along with the caption "FISH LIFE".

"Who are you?" I asked.

"I," he intoned, "am the Indescribable Horror."

I blinked. Several times.

"I don't mean to be rude, but you're actually highly describable."

His face darkened with anger. "This mortal shell is but a flesh disguise. Flimsy and disposable. It means nothing! My true self lies within, and none can describe the depth of the blackness of my essence!"

The terrible thing within me that made me write slashfic at work stirred. "How black is it?"

"It is blacker than the night, blacker than pitch, blacker than a starless sky! Blacker than the despair of a man upon the gallows! Blacker than the spawn of Shub-Niggurath! Blacker than the blackest licorice jelly bean!"

"That is very black," I agreed. "But also quite describable."

And that's when he threw me into the quarry.

Like my job loss, I'd expected it, and planned to swim for the beach on the opposite shore. But the water was shockingly cold, and so I gasped and floundered as he whipped off his fancy robe and dove in after me.

We struggled. I'm not sure for how long. I've always been a pretty good swimmer, but the Indescribable Horror was nimble as a minnow, and soon he had my arms pinned and was dragging us both down. Questions flitted through my mind, as I said, concerning Chewie and my husband and my ongoing consumption of frog pee…but I also wondered if there was an afterlife. Would I become a ghost, my restless spirit eternally bound to this quarry? Would my ghost ever get tired of watching skinny-dippers and couples making out in the bushes? I considered my taste in fanfic and realized: no, it probably wouldn't get tired of it.

Abruptly, Indescribable released me as though some invisible force had snatched him away. As I kicked sputtering to the surface, another pair of hands, gentle as the breath of a unicorn, took hold of the sleeve of my windbreaker and led me back to shore.

It was too dark to see my benefactor there in the quarry, but as I staggered onto the pebbles, coughing up water, I saw two insanely ripped, sopping wet shirtless men putting zip tie cuffs on Indescribable. Other exceptionally buff men in rainbow fatigues were chasing cultists through the trees and erasing the eldritch ritual symbols.

"Thank you," I gasped.

"No, thank *you*," the taller of the shirtless men replied. "We knew the ritual was going down but we didn't have enough intel to identify the location. You provided exactly what we needed."

"You got here super-fast!"

"We always come quickly," his companion replied. "When appropriate."

"Dr. Tingle sends his regards, by the way." The first man handed me my cell phone. "And suggests that perhaps you should try your pen at writing erotica professionally."

"Really? He doesn't think the market is over-saturated by now?"

"Smut is like Jell-O at Thanksgiving," he said. "There's always room for more!"

"You smell like frogs," Pete complained sleepily as I slipped into bed beside him.

"I'm sure it's just your imagination, dear."

"You went out, didn't you?"

"Why would I go out at this hour?" I pulled the comforters up around my chin.

"Because of the crazy cult stuff we saw on TV?"

"That seems far-fetched, doesn't it?"

"I don't actually hear you denying any of this," he pointed out.

I fell silent, my cheeks heating in the darkness, waiting for him to tell me what big dummy I was.

He sighed and hugged me close. "I'm just glad you're okay."

"I love you." I stroked his hair.

"Did love save the day?"

"It always does."

Publication History

"Beggars' Night"—*Halloween: New Poems*, Cemetery Dance Publications, May 2010.

"Hazelnuts and Yummy Mummies"—*Behold! Oddities, Curiosities and Undefinable Wonders*, Crystal Lake Publishing, July 2017.

"Cosmic Cola"—*What October Brings: A Lovecraftian Celebration of Halloween*, Celaeno Press, September 2018.

"Visions of the Dream Witch"—*A Secret Guide to Fighting Elder Gods*, Pulse Publishing, April 2019.

"What Dwells Within"—*Shadowed Souls*, Penguin Random House, November 2016.

"The Porcupine Boy"—*The Porcupine Boy and Other Anthological Oddities*, Crossroad Press, 2019.

"In the Family"—*Tales From The Lake Vol. 5*, Crystal Lake Publishing, November 2018.

"The Kind Detective"—*Ashes and Entropy*, Nightscape Press, December 2018.

"A Preference For Silence"—*Lady Churchill's Rosebud Wristlet*, Issue #5, November 1999.

"Wake Up Naked Monkey You›re Going To Die"—*War on Christmas: An Anthology of Tinseled Mayhem*, ChiZine Publications, October 2019.

"The Great VüDü Teen Linux Zombie Massacree"—*Funny Horror*, UFO Publishing, February 2017.

"The House That Couldn't Clean Itself"—*ROBOTS! Origins Game Fair Anthology*, Rio Grande Games, June 2016.

"The Toymaker's Joy"—*Naughty or Nice: A Holiday Anthology*, Evil Girlfriend Media, November 2015.

"The Tingling Madness"— *The Cackle of Cthulhu*, Baen Books, January 2018.

About the Author

Lucy A. Snyder is the five-time Bram Stoker Award-winning and Shirley Jackson Award-nominated author of over 100 published short stories and 14 books. Chaosium will release her novel *The Girl With the Star-Stained Soul* sometime in 2021. She also wrote the novels *Spellbent, Shotgun Sorceress*, and *Switchblade Goddess*, the nonfiction book *Shooting Yourself in the Head for Fun and Profit: A Writer's Survival Guide*, and the collections *Garden of Eldritch Delights, While the Black Stars Burn, Soft Apocalypses, Orchid Carousals, Sparks and Shadows, Chimeric Machines*, and *Installing Linux on a Dead Badger*. Her writing has been translated into French, Russian, Italian, Spanish, Czech, and Japanese editions and has appeared in publications such as *Asimov's Science Fiction, Apex Magazine, Nightmare Magazine, Pseudopod, Strange Horizons*, and *Best Horror of the Year*.

With Michael Bailey, Lucy also co-edited the critically-acclaimed collaborative dark fiction anthology *Chiral Mad 4*. When she's not writing, she's faculty in Seton Hill University's MFA program in Writing Popular Fiction and also works as a freelance developmental editor in a suburb of Columbus, Ohio. You can learn more about her at www.lucysnyder.com and you can follow her on Twitter at @LucyASnyder.